TO

AKILLA family

with best wishes

Sriniva~

Jan 1, 2009

Adventures of Andreux
Book One: Aranya

by

S. Pabbaraju

iUniverse, Inc.
New York   Bloomington

Adventures of Andreux

Book One - Aranya

iUniverse books may be ordered through booksellers or by contacting:

iUniverse
1663 Liberty Drive
Bloomington, IN 47403
www.iuniverse.com
1-800-Authors (1-800-288-4677)

ISBN: 978-0-595-40964-8 (pbk)
ISBN: 978-1-4401-0075-8 (cloth)
ISBN: 978-0-595-85323-6 (ebk)

Printed in the United States of America

iUniverse rev. date: 11/18/08

*To Nymisha
with love*

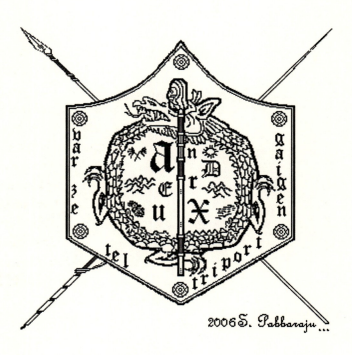

2006 S. Pabbaraju ...

Preface

To ponder that the credit for this entire story must rest with me makes me restless. I have to share with you the names and contributions of various people who have so graciously, willingly, knowingly or unknowingly and otherwise have contributed to this story. This story has, after all, been in the making for almost 20 years.

What started off as an innocent story-writing competition in the final year of college became an all-consuming passion in the years that followed. The first version of the story was in Telugu, my native language, and had a lot of colourful illustrations. I had written about 32 pages when I submitted the draft for initial review by a lecturer in my college. The only other contender was my close friend, Shyam Kumar Avvari, whom I have always considered a better storyteller than me. However, the results were never known, nor were the stories returned to us. What happened to them still remains a mystery to both of us.

After that, though I had made two or three more attempts to rewrite the story, I found I could not write beyond the 32nd page. I suppose I had developed a mental block of sorts. As time passed, my life became too busy to work on my story. With a wife, a newborn daughter, full-time work and full-time studying, I felt that my story would have to wait. But it was fresh in my mind all through the years.

Then my daughter, Nymisha, started to read storybooks. She loved to read all sorts of books. Stories of kings, queens, magic and princesses were her favourite. It so happened one night that I started to narrate the *Adventures of Andreux* to her as a bedtime story. She seemed very interested, and she was excited to know that it was my story. It began as a much-abridged version of the story told here, but Nymisha would not let me stop where I had once let myself do so. Therefore, I had to narrate the entire story to her over the next few months. I also had to make the story interesting enough that it would maintain her curiosity. Thus I successfully overcame the hurdle of the 32nd page. The character of Pompompulous, who became one of the main characters as a result of Nymisha's influence, was originally a five-scene character! Glimp was not even mentioned in the first draft. Nymisha has pointed out several mistakes and loopholes in my story with all the enthusiasm and honesty of a child, which helped me immensely while I made the final changes.

But there is much more to the story than the story itself. Many people have influenced me, my reading habits and my literary style, and thus have influenced the tone, texture and contents of this book as well.

My grandfather, the late Dr. Kameswara Rao Jayanthi, who taught me to read and write in such a unique way and has left the most significant impression on me with his literary skills and unassuming, kind nature; my parents, Mr. Subba Rao Pabbaraju and Dr. Saraswathi Pabbaraju, who always believed in me and my skills and sent me off to the best possible school that I could ever wish to go to (though I am sure it restricted their budget a bit, it never dampened their resolve); my aunt Dr. C. Ananda Ramam, who significantly influenced my writing skills and moulded my interest in Telugu literature with her wonderfully realistic novels; my cousins Dr. Padmaja and Dr. Sailaja for introducing me to the mysterious world of Agatha Christie; my aunt Dr. Syamala Rao, who tweaked my interest in solving crosswords; Satish Maryala, my friend with whom I had long and endless discussions about stories filled with magic and fantasy; my Telugu teacher, Mr. T. Ramachandra Rao, who believed in my writing and editing skills and gave me the opportunity to work as a contributor and editor for the school magazine; Mr. Puranik, my geography teacher, who introduced me to map drawing (without omitting the smallest of details) when he drew the map of the prison compound while narrating the story of *The Great Escape*; my dearest friend, Shyam Kumar Avvari, who has remained the single most inspiring person in my life, for everything and above all, for pushing me to more than I thought was my maximum capacity; my cousin Chandrasekhar Pemmaraju, who was always eager and enthusiastic to listen to my stories and songs; my wife Kanti Pabbaraju, who showed me what kindness, understanding and good character were, and without whose help and support this book would not be a reality (Thank you for showing me that you believed in me and for letting me drift away into my fantasies while you toiled hard!); and finally, my daughter, Nymisha, with whom I have spent countless hours, days and nights reading several other stories and discussing Andreux. She has not only come up with the names of most of my characters, but also helped me crystallize some of the fundamental concepts in the story. God bless them all!

This list would not be complete without adding a special tribute to my mother. While my grandfather laid the foundation for my reading and writing and my daughter motivated me to write this story, the enormous gap between these two phases in my life was bridged because of my mother. She has not only taught me good from bad, she taught me to be better. Without her active involvement in my life, I cannot imagine what type of human being I would have ended up being. She has been and will always be my friend, philosopher and guide. This book is an homage of sorts to my mother and all mothers in the world.

And then there are several authors and publication agencies whose works have satisfied my literary urges all these years. They not only kept my mind active with their published work, but also motivated me to write my own story. I have been influenced by them in more ways than one: in plot development, establishing characters, creating subtle descriptions that add *oomph* to an otherwise dull story and knowing when to end a particular scene while still keeping the reader's attention. These are too many to name here and I humbly salute them for their literary endeavours.

My sincere thanks to iUniverse, for their belief in me and for bringing this project to ink and paper. I had the most wonderful time in writing this book and sincerely hope you will equally enjoy reading it. With these words, I now retreat back to the storyboard to work on the next part of the adventures. Thanks once again.

S. Pabbaraju

June 2, 2008

Just a Little Bit of This and That

If time were a riddle, then here is the key
that wipes off the smudges, makes it clear to see.
For all those questions that you have for me,
read on, wait no more, and you will be free.

Let me attempt to explain the background and social settings and principles that existed at the time(s) when this story occurred.

Though the adventures of Andreux took place on our very own Earth, it was several thousands of years ago (several hundred hogashes, to be precise). Thus it has several points of interest that are quite unique compared to our modern-day facts, usages and beliefs. All of the information contained here may not be relevant for 'Aranya', but have a signicant bearing on the story that follows.

To start with, time is the chief factor in this story—time that always changes and yet never brings attention to itself. As you read, you will notice that a lot of words that describe time are quite different from the words you and I know. In order to make the story more authentic and representative of its times, I have used these certain terms of time measurement in attempting to chronicle Andreux's adventures. I could have easily approximated or equated them with modern-day terms such as morning, afternoon, month and year. However, that would have stripped the story of its uniqueness, and to narrate it otherwise would not do it justice. So it was with much apprehension that I rewrote parts of this book. However, to my utter amazement, I found it simple enough to stick to the then-used time measures. (The only problem I now face is that I can no longer relate to the time measures that we use these days!)

Anyway, without much further ado, here are a few of the words that I have generously borrowed from Andreux's time. While the common folk spoke to each other in *Viridi*, magic was taught in *Bedouni*. Black magic on the other hand was scriptured in a rare language, *Vishuchi*. You will do well to understand these terms from Viridi. . Here, I have tried to explain them just as Hermitus would have to his disciples.

Days and nights were not created equal. They changed with weather patterns and seasons. There were three main seasons: *oppressive heat, downpour* and *bitter cold*—the names of which are self-evident, of course. In between each season was a transient semi-season, which was often referred to as *fair weather*. In oppressive heat, days were longer than nights. In bitter cold, on the other hand, nights lasted longer than days. The duration of days and nights were measured using the sun as a reference point.

Though a day was measured with reference to the sun, everything else was measured with reference to the moon. The period covering the days from no moon to full moon was called *high lune* (*lune* meant "of or relating to moon"). The period covering the days from full moon to no moon was called *low lune*. Two consecutive lunes constituted a *meth* (or "moon cycle"). And thirteen meths made a *yedib*. Thus a yedib, based on modern-day calculations had 390 days compared to 365 or 366 days. Oppressive heat, downpour and bitter cold lasted three meths each, whereas fair-weathers were always a meth long. There was one extra meth during a yedib, which was added to any one main season depending upon the relative positions of sun and moon. There were floods every twelve yedibs, and thus a twelve-yedib period was referred to as a *hogash* (*hog* meaning "fill with" and *gash* meaning "source of water").

The average time a human being took to blink one's eyes was called a *monnet* (*mon* meaning "eye" and *net* meaning "close"). Though it has no direct bearing on measurement of days or nights, the expression is used frequently to describe how fast or slow one's reflexes were in reacting or responding to a situation.

Moving on to other things, people used gold, silver and copper coins as monetary units of trade. Each kingdom had its own types of coins for internal trade. Coins with royal insignia were used to settle trade between two kingdoms. A kingdom's prosperity was measured in terms of the number of coins that were in circulation in the kingdom at a given point in time, which depended on whether or not there were trade surpluses. Every kingdom maintained an army of mighty warriors, not only to safeguard its own borders and subjects, but also to loot and plunder neighbouring kingdoms. Gold was the most valuable, and it was therefore no surprise that dragons also plundered cities and treasuries to steal gold coins, which they saved and guarded in their caves.

There were two types of dragons. Some of them were ordinary dragons (though let me warn you, there is nothing ordinary about any dragon!), while some were magical and powerful. An ordinary dragon was born as a dragon and lived and died as one. Whereas an average human being lived for five hogashes, a dragon lived for fourteen hogashes. A dragon, when it stood on all of its six feet, would measure up to three human beings standing one on top of the other. A dragon had a long, slithering and coiled body with three pairs of legs and a tiny pair of wings that helped it to take off and descend. The legs had toenails that were longer than your modern-day utility knives and cut much deeper. A dragon's tongue always spit fire and its eyes were always blood-red, which had nothing to do with it being angry or not. A dragon had three rows of sharp and serrated teeth. The body was full of hard metallic scales that were impenetrable to arrows, swords and spears. However, there were magic spells that would weaken the resistance of such scales and, when used with sharp weapons, would easily kill a dragon. There were, however, no spells that would kill a dragon without the use of any weapons. The ordinary dragons were mostly found around the Vauntic Sea, and they terrorized people living in nearby villages and cities.

The magical and powerful dragons lived in the caves near the Uldric Sea. It was next to impossible to travel to these caves. The turbulent sea waters mostly managed to kill the travelers. Those that survived the sea were then subjected to the harsh and powerful spells of the dragons that lived nearby. It was extremely rare to find a human being who lived to tell his experiences with the dragons that flew over Uldric Sea.

These dragons learnt magic, not the normal day-to-day magic that we (do not) see every day. They were the followers of the Lord of Evil and Darkness that were expelled out of their homes during the reign of the Trinity. Most of them were human beings, witches, wizards and ogres that practiced dark magic, the type of magic that involved torture and death. When expelled, they transformed themselves into dragons and fled to the Uldric Sea, which was beyond the reach of the powers of the Trinity.

In the human realm, justice was severe and harsh. There was practically no mercy for the guilty. Once accused, it was up to the accused to prove his or her innocence. When found guilty, the punishment was generally "an eye for an eye"—the guilty had to suffer the same loss as the victim. Although this basic principle almost always prevailed, each ruler had a slightly different interpretation of the rules, which made them more flexible in meting out punishments

There were, of course, no banks at that time. The kings had large treasuries, guarded day and night by several guards and further fortified to prevent unauthorized access. Common folk, however, had to use their ingenuity to hide their savings. Often they would fill up pots with their gold or copper and bury them underground inside their dwellings. Some of them would bury them under forest trees or in caves, which was riskier due to the potential losses caused by natural calamities. Those with supernatural powers used them well to protect their riches. There were no taxes, only tolls whenever people crossed the tollgates at the entrance of each kingdom. It was very expensive to produce coins, and therefore there were not a lot of them in circulation at any given point in time. Thus, people mostly resorted to bartering wherever possible.

There was a lot of discrimination (which I do not support at all, but have to report in this story to maintain the integrity of the narration), based on caste and creed. It was common for the rich people to maintain slaves and servants, who were often ill-treated. While slaves had no rights of freedom whatsoever, servants were a little better off. They were free and worked for measly payments. Slaves were distinguished from servants or other free folk by permanent tattoos on their forehead. The tattoo was usually a symbol that represented his or her owner. A person born to a slave had to lead a slave's life. A slave could become a free folk if freedom was granted by the owner. A free folk could become a slave when faced with poverty.

Schools were then called *tutelages*, teachers were *masters* and students were *disciples*. Disciples were sent off to learn from masters at their tutelages when they were young. The disciples lived at the tutelage (similar to boarding schools these days). Some of the tutelages were quite far off from where a disciple lived, so they did not often get to visit their family once they went off to learn. There were also two types of tutelages. Some tutelages, where families had to pay to enroll their children, were posh and pompous and often out of the reach of common folk. Royal descendants and children of affluent parents went there to learn. It would, however, be a misconception to consider these as better tutelages. Bigger and richer is not always better, you see! The other type of tutelage was where the master taught for free. The master would select the disciple based on one's potential and capabilities.

Not many children enrolled in tutelages, as they had to help their parents earn a livelihood. Those that enrolled stayed at the tutelage until their master decided that they had completed their education. The more common subjects that were taught were life vitals (what we refer to as science), language, herbimedics (medicine for the common man), fine arts, physical well-being and stargazing. Some masters, such as Hermitus, taught magic and spells to those whom they perceived to be deserving of such knowledge. There were some other tutelages (very rare to find), where the masters taught exclusively dark magic. Disciples usually had to make physical, social or spiritual sacrifices to show their commitment before they were accepted in such tutelages.

There are several other colloquial terms that have been used in the book, for which definitions have been given as they appear. These are easy to understand and as they do not relate to the general background, have not been discussed here.

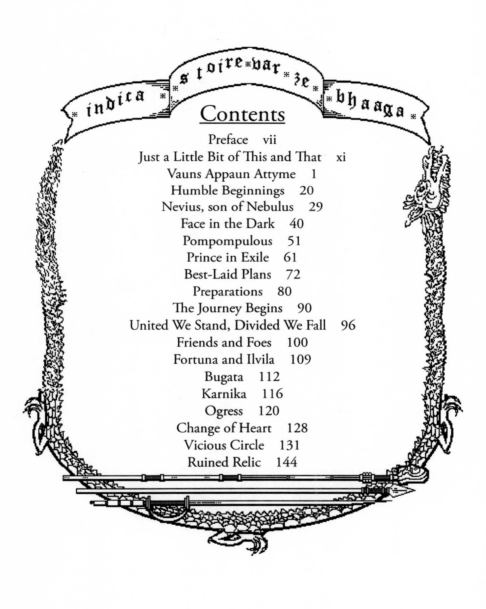

Contents

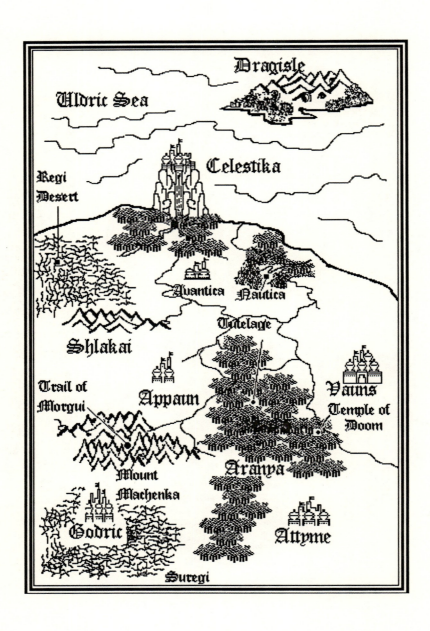

Prologue
Vauns Appaun Attyme

What happened one night when the world was but still
will come back to haunt, the memories will chill.
From under the seas and over the hill,
the evil will creep and come back to kill.

Of all the tasks that King Vermaintt assigned to Vegu, this was by far the most dangerous one. A small mistake could cost him his life. However, he knew this task was more important. Two days ago, the king had warned him that the future of Vauns depended on the message that he would bring back. Vegu walked gingerly in Aranya, the dark and dense jungle that stretched out west of the kingdom.

His Majesty King Vermaintt had explained to Vegu that he had learnt that his opponent Levitor had sought refuge in the Ruined Relics, an old temple ruined by the savages and the efflux of time, embedded in Aranya. There had been sightings of half-world creatures moving in the vicinity, which forewarned imminent danger. Vermaintt had sent Vegu to get concrete evidence of Levitor's presence in Aranya.

The silence that surrounded him was eerie and uncomfortable. The darkness was so dense that he could cut it with a knife. The *lepana* (ointment) that his Master gave him to see in darkness, wore off a little while ago. As he inched through the jungle, he thought he heard a faint noise. He stopped in his tracks, which caused his messenger pigeon, painted in black, to tighten its hold on his shoulder.

Vegu stopped and tried to look further into the darkness that engulfed him. The quiet was deceptive. He could not see the hungry black eyes of the half-world creature perched in a nearby tree in the guise of a python. Nor could he see the glimmer of light from the ruined relic a little farther away.

As he took a few more steps, Vegu's black bird dug its claws into his shoulder. Sensing danger, Vegu stopped and glanced around. Just as he

1

began to move forward again, the python fell from the tree, crushing him under its weight. Vegu tore into the snake with his dagger, but the python was already beginning to coil around him. The pigeon, trained for such emergencies, released its grip and flew away into the night. Vegu fought valiantly as the python entwined him, breaking a few of Vegu's ribs. The spy yelled in immense agony. Just as the python was about to crush him completely, Vegu heard a faint voice from afar.

"Get him here to me, alive."

The python's grip loosened.

"Yes, my master," the half-world creature said, resuming its original form. Vegu could vaguely see a black shape in the darkness, but its features were not clear. As the creature caught Vegu in its firm grip, Vegu barely managed to remain conscious. His body was damaged beyond repair.

As the creature dragged his body to the ruined relic, Vegu caught a glimpse of Levitor, his master's arch-nemesis.

"Who do we have here?" growled Levitor as he approached Vegu. Levitor looked at Vegu intently, but it did not appear that he recognized the intruder.

"He is a spy, Master." The half-world creature's voice was screechy and unbearable. "I have been following him for some time. He was looking for someone or something."

"Is that right!" Levitor's voice resounded in the ruins. "What were you spying on? Or rather, who were you spying for?" he asked. Vegu remained quiet as he looked around to take in as many details as possible. Levitor's face reddened with impatience. He walked towards Vegu with giant steps.

"Answer me!" He slapped Vegu with brutal force. Vegu coughed and vomited blood at the impact. He remained silent.

"Did Vermaintt send you to spy on me?" Levitor shouted again. Vegu showed no recollection of his master's name.

"Take this insolent creature away. I will get the truth from him very soon. If I do not succeed, I will feed him to the spirits. I need to make sure I am fully prepared for tomorrow's ritual," he ordered the half-world creature, and then he walked away.

Vegu heard Levitor walking into the next room and muttering, "I cannot afford these little setbacks to upset my plans for tomorrow night. I must remain focused."

Vegu struggled to stand as the half-world creature dragged him to a nearby pillar. As his hands were tied behind the pillar, Vegu hoped for a moment of privacy in order to scribble a message for his pigeon. He knew that it was waiting somewhere nearby for his orders.

The half-world creature finished tying Vegu's hands and legs to the pillar and took a few steps. It sat facing him and Vegu could clearly see its features in the dim light that shone in the relic.

The creature wore dirty, loose garb, and its unkempt hair smelled foul. Its skin was pale white, and its eyes lacked life and shone like glass pebbles. Vegu could clearly see the bones in its hands as if skin had been patched directly onto them, without any flesh in between. Vegu closed his eyes, unable to view the repulsive creature any more.

He then heard a small noise. It was faint but familiar. It was the fluttering of his pigeon's wings. The noise distracted the half-world creature, and it went looking for the source of the sound.

Vegu seized the opportunity and managed to untie his hands with little difficulty. With one hand, he grabbed his dagger and with the other, he pulled out a piece of parchment from his cummerbund. He slit his hand with the dagger and scribbled hurriedly on the parchment. "Darkness looms … Doom awaits bluemoon night … no time to lose …" As he heard the approaching footsteps, he threw the parchment out the window.

"What are you doing?" The half-world creature looked at him suspiciously. Its eyes narrowed when it saw that his hands were free and that his hand was bleeding.

"How did you manage to do that?" As the half-world creature approached him, Vegu saw a faint movement from the corner of his eye. His pigeon had gotten his message. Just then, he heard Levitor's voice reverberate in the relics.

"Finish him off once and for all; he will be of no use to us, that impertinent nuisance."

The half-world creature's eyes gleamed in sadistic pleasure as it resumed its python form. As Vegu's bones crushed under its tightened grip, a whisper escaped his lips. "Sorry, my master."

Vermaintt gazed out his chamber windows at the sunset. The chamber stood on the topmost floor of a stone castle that had been built about a hogash ago. From its top, Vermaintt could see the borders of the neighbouring Appauntic and Attymine kingdoms.

He was troubled by the fact that it had been two days since his trusted spy, Vegu, had set out to Aranya to find out about the presence of Levitor in Aranya. *It is quite unlike him not to contact me,* Vermaintt thought. *It was no doubt an exceptionally dangerous task, but Vegu had accepted the risk when he set out to accomplish it.* The sun was slowly dropping out of sight, and Vermaintt noticed a few dark clouds that lingered. In front of the clouds he noticed the silhouette of a bird. The bird's arrival confirmed Vegu's death. It held a scroll of parchment in its legs, on which the spy had scribbled what he had witnessed shortly before his death.

"Darkness looms … Doom awaits bluemoon night … no time to lose …" The letters were barely legible, but its message was clear. Levitor was in Aranya.

Realizing the gravity of the situation, Vermaintt sent telepathic messages to Tentaculus and Magnolia, with whom he had formed the Pact of Trinity two hogashes ago, when they were all disciples of Grandel-Fiore, the wizard of wizards. The danger might be averted if they acted fast, Vermaintt cautioned them, as Levitor was unaware his secret mission had been leaked out by a swift pigeon. The spy indicated that Levitor had plans for bluemoon night, which was tonight. And they had much to achieve in that short span of time.

Dusk was settling over the kingdom and birds flew overhead in hundreds to reach their nests before darkness engulfed the skies. It was not safe for any human or beast to venture out in the darkness when creatures of the half-world roamed freely to feast on unsuspecting wanderers.

Tentaculus had been swift to respond to the message, but Vermaintt still had not heard from Her Highness Queen Magnolia. Vermaintt briefly recollected all the yedibs that the three friends had struggled and laboured in creating their kingdoms, all the lives lost, all the sacrifices made and all the pains endured in ensuring the well-being of their subjects. It had taken them a half-hogash to build the rock castle alone. The impregnable fortress had witnessed many labourers crushed and buried alive under the monstrous weight of the rocks used in its construction. All those sacrifices would be worthless if they lost their kingdoms now. And they had until midnight. Vermaintt stirred uneasily in his chair. What was keeping Magnolia from contacting him? he wondered.

Looking up from his thoughts, Vermaintt saw a bright purple star glowing in the sky above the Attymine Kingdom. *Tentaculus must be getting impatient,* he thought, *sending signals from his wand for me to see.* He could not blame him. Magnolia had never been in his good books, had she? She and Tentaculus remained on talking terms only because of Vermaintt's frequent interventions. Tentaculus was a very meticulous man, never leaving anything to chance. Magnolia, on the other hand, was intuitive and carefree. Vermaintt, the visionary among them, believed that if the three of them remained bound by their Pact of Trinity, no force would be able to harm them, not even Levitor. As a matter of fact, they had no choice but to be united in order to survive. As long as they remained united, their power of Trinity guarded them from Levitor, who was rejected by Venetia, Vermaintt's wife.

What a difference a woman could make in the lives of two men! he thought, remembering the day his wife, Venetia, had chosen him as her husband, thwarting Levitor's attempts to woo her. When confronted by Levitor, Venetia had told him in plain words that she had chosen Vermaintt and nothing would change her mind. He might capture her body, but that was all that he would get, she had cautioned him. Her heart would always belong to Vermaintt. But Levitor, who thought himself to be the first among equals and the best in skills, claimed that he could not understand what Venetia saw in the pathetic excuse for life that Vermaintt was. Levitor had not been able to deal with her rejection and promised deadly consequences for the betrayal. It was

Venetia's decision that drove Levitor to the half-world. It came as no surprise to the Trinity that a short time later, the broken arrow was declared the heir-apparent to the Lord of Evil and Darkness. She was the reason why Levitor was who he was now.

But now that was going to change. If the Trinity did not act fast, with his act of self-sacrifice, Levitor would gain supremacy over Earth. After that, nothing would matter. Vermaintt knew he would be better off dead than Levitor's captive.

Vermaintt's thoughts were interrupted by the sound of faint footsteps and the tinkling of dainty anklet bells in his chamber. He turned to see the familiar face of his beloved wife, Venetia, Queen of Vauns. She was walking slowly, holding their newborn son in her arms. Her blue, soulful eyes were gleaming with happiness. Vermaintt recollected the first time he had seen her; she had had the same poise and elegance. The yedibs had only added to her grace and dignity.

"My dear! You shouldn't have come so far by yourself. You should have called for me," said Vermaintt as he got up from his chair near the window and walked towards her. Her face was glowing like a full moon.

"Do not worry about me. I am recovering fine and according to dear old Celesta, I should be in perfect health by the end of this lune. But how are you? Is everything going according to the plan?" She handed their child to Vermaintt. The king looked at his son. His eyes grew moist with pride. He would do everything possible to pass on his kingdom to his son. He kissed him on the forehead and placed him in Venetia's arms. He was again filled with hope. "I am known to be an eternal optimist. There is no reason why that should change now," he said.

"I am glad to hear that. As long as you have hope, the god will be with you. And remember, you will always have me, no matter what happens," she said as he bent to kiss her. She looked at him passionately and then walked out of the chamber.

King Vermaintt returned to the window and looked up at the sky. There was not much time left. He walked to the mighty oak door, which was carved with intricate lions and dragons. He pointed the emerald ring on his right-hand index finger at the door and chanted

"*Var ze Gaigen tel Triport!*" The door disappeared, revealing a shining metal casket that stood upright. The casket had no locks or knobs or handles. Instead, Vermaintt opened it by waving his hand in the air. Inside was a magnificent black metal shield that shone like a mirror.

The shield was engraved with a lion standing on its hind legs. There were rubies in the place of the lion's eyes, which made it look angry. The lion's front legs held a beautifully sculpted sceptre, embedded with jewels. Vermaintt looked at the sceptre and the royal insignia that symbolized the Vauntic Kingdom. It reminded him of the day his father told him the significance of the sceptre.

When Vermaintt was young, he had not been a prince. The Kingdom of Vauns had not existed then. When Vermaintt had been three hogashes old, he had founded it. Nambul, the enchanted sceptre, which now adorned the royal shield, had been given to Vermaintt by his father, who in turn had received it from his father. Legend had it that the sceptre had been handed down to fifteen generations before it had come to Vermaintt.

The sceptre was made of a substance not found within the realms of the living. Many scholars and researchers had tried and failed to identify the substance. The thick, long staff was embedded with rare and precious jewels. At the tip of the staff was the head of a lion, magnificently sculpted out of gold. Even more impressive was its power. In the hands of its rightful master, a true descendant of Vermaintt's lineage, the sceptre bore unlimited magical powers. If one turned the head of the lion to its right, a powerful torch would emerge from the sceptre that could heal any scar or wound, making the holder invincible against all human weapons. Also when its bearer was lost in an unknown place, the sceptre would point to the right direction.

Such an enchanted sceptre came with its price though. It had to be respected as if it represented the god himself. It had to be guarded from all evil influences. In the absence of safekeeping by its rightful master, the sceptre would weaken. After one and one-half hogashes of such neglect (as supposedly calculated by an astrologer, based on the positions of the sun, the moon and the stars in relation to the horoscope of Vermaintt's lineage), the sceptre would return to its divinity and

---

1 In Bedouni, this means "By the Order of Trinity."

would only return to the descendants upon the performance of certain next-to-impossible tasks.

Vermaintt bowed to the shield in reverence and placed it on a rug, made of wool from llamas that roamed freely in the hills of Shlakai, which was thrown across the round bronze table. He closed his eyes and waved his hand at the exits to his chamber, locking them all at once. His mind was chanting the spell *'Pravidita'* that would reveal the images that one desired to see. *"Mam dir Mam vidir"*[2]

Each of the three mighty rulers had an identical shield, that they had created to forge their power, for times of duress and emergency. As Vermaintt chanted, the shield was transformed into a mirror and the image of Queen Magnolia appeared on it.

He could see her pacing back and forth in her chamber. The huge walls, typical of Appauntic heritage and tradition, displayed elaborate architectural design. The queen was tall; her sharp features and small black eyes belied her carefree nature. Yet Vermaintt noticed her face showed signs of anxiety. With pursed lips and eyebrows tied in a knot, she looked towards the entrance to her chamber as if she were expecting a visitor. The dark purplish robes that she was wearing made her skin look ghostly white.

Whom is she waiting for? Did she forget our fates will be sealed if we do not act fast? thought Vermaintt. Then he saw something in the mirror that heightened his curiosity.

Vermaintt saw a black-robed figure, whose face was covered by a hood, approaching Magnolia. As the figure drew nearer to her, the tension in Magnolia's face increased.

"What took you so long?" she asked. "You know we do not have enough time."

"I am sorry for the delay, Your Highness Queen Magnolia. But I had to take every precaution to make sure that I was not followed," said the figure. Vermaintt tried to recollect whose voice it was but could not. He waited, hoping to see the stranger's face.

"We need to hurry. Give me Degamur!" commanded Magnolia.

"Before I do that, I need to know you will keep your promise after tonight," demanded the stranger.

---

2 I see what I desire

"This is not the time for this discussion," said Magnolia, her hand stretched to receive the sword from the stranger.

"I will not give you the sword!" yelled the stranger, and he removed the hood. The stranger was General Trecherus, Magnolia's chief army commander. *Why had Magnolia delegated the task of retrieving the sword to him, of all persons! She should have been more careful.* Vermaintt clenched his fists as he continued to watch. If they managed to complete their scheduled task before midnight, he would be having a long chat with her. His gaze returned to the shield once again.

"Too bad. Then you will have to bear the consequences," said Magnolia. She raised her right hand and snapped her fingers. A wand appeared in her hand.

Trecherus appeared unperturbed. He pulled the sword from under his robes and pointed it at her. "While I was returning to your chamber, I had the presence of mind to read the inscription on the sword. As long as I hold this sword in my hand, none of your magic will work on me." He gave a wicked laugh. Magnolia looked at him with contempt.

Vermaintt was growing impatient.

"So how was your meeting with Emperor Vernaculus?" asked Trecherus, obviously enjoying the moment.

"He never showed up." Magnolia spoke through a clenched jaw, and Vermaintt could tell she was seething with anger.

"Well, well. Everything has worked according to my plan, hasn't it!"

Magnolia glowered at him. "You sent me the message that Emperor Vernaculus wanted to meet with me urgently, didn't you! Just so you could retrieve Degamur. Oh, how I wish I had listened to Vermaintt and Tentaculus!"

"Very good Queen Magnolia! I'm impressed. Quick, but unfortunately not quick enough." He walked menacingly towards her with the sword in his hand.

"You do not understand. Give me the sword before it is too late. I need the sword to protect my kingdom," Magnolia replied.

"Ah! Your kingdom! Very soon it will be *my* kingdom."

Magnolia moved back. Even though her magic was powerless against the sword, the power of Trinity was still very powerful. She held her wand high and shouted: "Holders of the Trinity Pact! Join me now in condemning this traitor. *Reganora man degamur³!*"

"What are you doing?" Trecherus stepped back in disbelief.

A bright red band of light erupted out of her wand and touched the sword. Vermaintt quickly reached for his wand and chanted the spell. "*Reganora vetora degamur*"⁴Green light emerged from his wand. He could see in the shield that the green light had bonded with the red light. He was also relieved to see purple light touching the sword. *Tentaculus must also have been watching,* thought Vermaintt. When the three bands of light touched the sword, it caused a blinding spark of lightning in Queen Magnolia's chamber. Trecherus ran towards her, wild-eyed, attempting to kill her with the sword. But by the time he reached her, the sword had disappeared from his hand. He let out a weak cry when he saw the sword in the Queen's hand. He fell to the ground in supplication.

"Forgive me, Queen Magnolia. I was overcome with greed and lost my mind. I will never betray you again. I swear on my life," he said. Then a faint voice came from the sword.

"Magnolia! Ignore him. We have only a little time. We need to focus on more important things."

Before Trecherus could respond, Magnolia waved her wand and chanting '*Alsi metouver⁵*', turned him into stone. Then with a flick of her fingers, she locked all the entrances to her chamber.

"My apologies for the delay, King Vermaintt and King Tentaculus. Now let us deal with Levitor once and for all," she said as she held the sword in her right hand.

"I hope we have enough time, Magnolia. You might have just cost us our kingdoms. After all the yedibs of hardship, you choose to send Trecherus to retrieve Degamur!" The harsh voice of Tentaculus echoed in the chambers of Vermaintt and Magnolia.

"Let us not argue now, my friends. It is time to focus on the present," replied Vermaintt. Even though they were each in their own chambers,

---

3 Translates to 'Bring back to me Degamur'
4 Return Degamur to her.
5 The word *metouver* means "motionless". When used with various words as a part of a spell, it would yield distinct results. The word *alsi* means "stone" and the combination *alsi metouver* would cause one's opponent to turn into a statue.

separated by thousands of miles covered with dense jungles and deep canyons, it was as if they were standing together in the disciples' cottage at the tutelage of Grandel-Fiore "Start the proceedings, Vermaintt," said Tentaculus, glaring in Magnolia's direction.

Vermaintt cleared his throat. "Let me summarize what will happen. First we invoke the holy spirits to stop the sacrificial procedure. This will most likely result in combat with Levitor. In order to prevent us from distracting him, he will use the deadly spell Annihilus on us. We must remain focused to thwart his powers. Any slight lapses will yield deadly consequences. As soon as we succeed in opposing him, we must proceed immediately in breaking the evil powers within him and setting them free. They, in turn, will devour him. We must ensure that this devouring happens after midnight. If Levitor dies before midnight, then he will have made the sacrifice within the deadline. While the evil powers are busy tearing Levitor apart, we must destroy them before they find another human surrogate. Is it clear? Do either of you have any questions?"

Neither of them had any questions. Vermaintt held his sceptre and pointed it southwest. At the same time, Magnolia pointed her sword towards north and Tentaculus his spear, Ezimuth, towards southeast. Then they all chanted the spell at once:

> We, the holders of the Trinity Pact,
> Call upon the forces of nature to act
> before the lord of evil can rise
> and rob us of the earth, oceans and skies.
>
> We vow to preserve, protect and serve
> the kingdoms we rule and the people we love.
> Let our solitary powers combine
> when the chants of us three entwine.
>
> When the chants twine and the powers combine,
> reveal us a sign that is pure and divine.
> *Na matso metouver, dote la sa divine.*

Var ze Gaigen tel Triport, indica dora signe.[6]

Rid the world of all hatred, evil and scorn!
May the evil be dead before it is born!
Na matso metouver, dote la sa divine.
Var ze Gaigen tel Triport, indica dora signe.

As the spell resonated in their chambers, sparks erupted from their weapons. There was a tumult in the skies as lightning and thunder attacked the darkness. The disturbances resulted in an immense commotion; all birds and animals woke from their sleep and ran from their shelters. The noise was deafening. Soon it was pouring down rain. The waters in the seas began to rise rapidly, and there was seismic turbulence under the surface. The powerful chants of the three neighbouring rulers cast a bright light in the skies as if another sun were dawning.

The shield in front of Vermaintt now reflected the image of Levitor. Deep in Aranya, the dark and dense jungle that was centrally located between the three kingdoms, in the Ruined Relic, Levitor prepared to offer his own life to achieve immortality. His eyes remained closed as his lips chanted the immortality spell. He stood tall and lean, like a hungry lion. His hair was unkempt and it fell to his chest. His nails were long and crooked, as was his nose, which looked like it had been split in two at the bridge. The corpse of the jaguar killed as an offering to the evil forces of nature lay bleeding and motionless beneath him. There was absolute silence, barring some strange whispers of spirits every now and then.

As Levitor prepared for his self-sacrifice, the flash of light from the weapons of the Trinity appeared from nowhere and struck him on his chest. Its impact would have killed an ordinary man in an instant.

---

6 This phrase means "Do not let evil live, cause to occur such a divinity. By the Order of Trinity, indicate such a sign." The word *na* means "do not," *mal* means "evil" (and when used in combination with certain words, the *l* is dropped) and *tso* means "breathe." As noted before, *metouver* means "motionless." Other important words in the phrase include *dote,* which means "cause," *sa,* which is the verb "to occur," *indica,* meaning "indicate," *dora,* which can often mean "such," and, of course, *signe,* meaning "sign."

Levitor survived the torching light; however, his concentration was disturbed. His eyes rolled back in his head as he cast a spell. An invisible cage surrounded him to shield him from any further interruptions.

Vermaintt spoke first. "He might kill himself now. Queen Magnolia, turn him to stone!"

In her own kingdom, far from Levitor's lair, Magnolia pointed her sword to the sky and drew a cage in the air as her lips chanted spells. Then she quickly slashed the sword against the imaginary cage with one hand, while with the other, she waved her wand as she cast a spell to turn Levitor to stone. At the same time, Vermaintt and Tentaculus also waved their wands, and their powers combined as the spell hit Levitor. His protective cage ripped open, and he was turned to stone from the neck down. His face was distorted with rage, his head swung forcefully and his neck began to bleed.

Tentaculus, noticing the blood, panicked and shouted, "He is trying to kill himself. Turn his head to stone!" Magnolia tried to cast the spell, but she knew as well as the others that Levitor's head was immune to their spells.

"If you cannot turn his head to stone, may I suggest that you unstone his body, while we think of some other way to stop this sacrifice?" Vermaintt said, his voice tinged with frustration.

Magnolia broke the spell. As soon as he realized that he was free, Levitor waved his arms in a violent swing, and the powerful light spark emerging from the weapons of the three mighty rulers started to flow rapidly into his body. His body was jerking intensely with the entry of each light wave.

"What is he doing?" asked Magnolia.

"Either he is trying to kill himself, or he is trying to rid us of our powers," said Tentaculus.

Midnight was still a few moments away. Then Vermaintt did something that no one had expected. He shouted, "*Centenviore dela forciez collapsiore Levitoran, var ze Gaigen tel Triport!*" Magnolia and Tentaculus, almost impulsively, repeated the chants without pausing to ponder the consequences.

---

7 This is translated as "May our forces congregate to vanquish Levitor, by the Order of Trinity!"

With each repetition of the chant, Levitor grew weaker and smaller. He shrunk as he tried to chant his way out of their spell. He started to chant the Annihilus spell as he shrunk, but it was past midnight before he could finish it. As the last phrase of the spell escaped his lips, it was but a whisper. When the spell of the Trinity ended, he burst with a huge explosion. Blood splattered all over the ruins.

The mighty rulers were about to heave a sigh of relief when they noticed that where Levitor had stood on the pedestal, a gigantic and gruesome granite statue of him now stood. His face was hideous, and fire poured from his eyes and tongue. His tongue itself was made of two snakes, twisted and entwined. His limbs were not human, but those of the jaguar that he had sacrificed earlier. The body below his waist was not human either, but it was not that of any creature known to mankind. It was repugnant, filled with calluses and scales and what appeared to be insects crawling out of fresh wounds.

"What happened? Why did that statue spring up on the pedestal?" asked Magnolia.

"I am not sure. The spell should have killed him, and I am sure it did; his blood is everywhere as proof of it," said Vermaintt.

"What happened to the evil powers inside him? Why didn't we see them?" asked Tentaculus.

Vermaintt was thinking. *What would cause Levitor to reappear as a statue when he died? The pedestal ...*

"I think we have a problem," he said. He didn't know if he could voice his worst fears. It was possible that Levitor had won after all. "Do you remember Xorg?"

"The pedestal of suspended immortality, which grants life after death to those who die while standing on it? The pedestal created by our master, Grandel-Fiore, the wizard of wizards, to stop his wife from dying an untimely death? What about it?" asked Magnolia.

Vermaintt frowned. The mighty wizard Grandel-Fiore, who had taught the Trinity and their opponent, Levitor, had been one of a kind. No one had surpassed him at wizardry. When his wife, Chantelle, had been pregnant with their first child, Grandel-Fiore had noticed the signs of death written on her face. Desperate to keep her alive, the wizard had supposedly created a pedestal and had poured all his powers into it. The result had been Xorg, the magical pedestal that extended life for a calculated period of time if, while passing from life to death, one stood on it. The positioning of stars in the sky at the precise moment of that passing would determine the length of the extension. Grandel-Fiore had brought his wife back to life. In his anxiety, however, he had miscalculated the positioning of the stars and his wife had barely lived to deliver their child. Unable to overcome the grief, Grandel-Fiore had supposedly destroyed the pedestal long before the Trinity had become his disciples. But apparently the pedestal had not been destroyed after all. *How had it gotten into the hands of Levitor?* The question puzzled Vermaintt.

"Levitor was standing on it when I killed him," said Vermaintt. Tentaculus gasped in horror, and his face became pale. "That scheming swine! What happens now?"

"Our spell killed him, but it did not kill him," replied Vermaintt.

"Can you elaborate?"

"He was killed on that pedestal. Therefore, he transformed into a phase of suspended mortality, which means he is not yet dead. All his evil powers are trapped inside him. We cannot vanquish them until he returns to life again."

"How long do we have to wait before that happens?" asked Magnolia.

"Too long, I am afraid," said Vermaintt. "We may not live to see that day. Even our great-grandchildren may not live to see that moment. The span of the suspended mortality depends upon the exact time of death. Levitor was killed when the star Millennia shone brightly on the Uldric Sea. That gives him 77 hogashes less a yedib, to be precise."

The brief jubilation that danced in their hearts died quickly. "Seventy-seven hogashes!" Tentaculus sank onto his throne. His face turned gray and sullen. Defeat was written all over it.

"Don't lose heart, Tentaculus," said Vermaintt. "We have enough time to come up with a strategy to destroy Levitor before he rises again. We have also gained ample time to build our kingdoms, to eradicate the forces of evil and continue with our plans for peace. We still have hope."

"Hope!" laughed Tentaculus bitterly. "The only hope I have right now is that in the future no one will remember that the sinister legacy of Levitor was passed on to them by me, the founder of their kingdom!"

Magnolia raised her arms above her head. "Listen to Vermaintt, Lord Tentaculus! What has happened has happened. It is time to look to the future. Vanquishing Levitor was only half the strategy. We—"

Tentaculus cut her off. "We have not done that properly either. If only we were able to kill him. I would like to retire for the night, if there is nothing else for us to do tonight and if you will kindly permit me to." He snapped his fingers and lost contact with Magnolia and Vermaintt.

While they were still young, before they came to rule their kingdoms, they had agreed that no communication would take place unless all three were present. Magnolia took leave as well, and Vermaintt was left to his own thoughts in his chamber. Peace returned to the skies once again.

The three rulers never did figure out a way to vanquish Levitor while they were alive. They focused their efforts on improving trade and farming. People lived peacefully in the kingdoms of the Trinity, and evil forces subsided into the background. As their leader had mysteriously vanished, the evil forces were easily dealt with. Under the able guidance of the Trinity, a gigantic mission was undertaken to cleanse their kingdoms of all evil. Unable to defend themselves against the merciless onslaught of the powerful rulers, the worshippers of the Lord of Evil and Darkness receded to the background. Most of them fled to the Uldric Sea, beyond the powers of the Trinity.

The statue of Levitor remained in Aranya, hidden in the Ruined Relic. As haunted tales cast a web of intrigue around the origin of the statue over the yedibs to come, the temple itself was slowly lost to the powers of nature, and it became hidden among the dense jungles of Aranya.

Many generations later, the story of Levitor was reduced to a mere fable. Mothers used his name to scare stubborn children. Because the tidings were good, the people overlooked the evil that was not visible to the naked eye. The kingdoms prospered under the peace accord between the three rulers. It was therefore no surprise that nothing happened in the next 75 hogashes that would have otherwise prevented Levitor from coming back to life and changing the course of this story.

PART ONE

AT THE TUTELAGE

The sky was clear blue; the grass was pure green.
Not much simpler could a story begin.
But when one man's envy exploded within,
it rattled the earth, skies and all that's between.

"Matunga!" Andreux shouted as he went looking for his master's deer that had inadvertently tiptoed into the forest. He stood tall and straight, his brown eyes searching for the animal. He had a spear in his hand, ready to attack any beast that might come in his way. With broad shoulders and a toned body, he was well developed for a young man who was just a few days shy of completing one and one-half hogashes. He looked around to gauge the situation.

The forest was dense with thick undergrowth of wild bushes and shrubs. The trees themselves were gigantic, and the branches of neighbouring trees were entwined to such an extent that they almost blocked out sunlight completely. Here and there, rays of sunshine peeked through as if it were raining light, and the trees, shrubs and leaves shone in delight. It was eerily quiet. The peace was unsettling, to say the least, and the naked eye could not distinguish between the prop roots hanging down the trees and the snakes twined around them.

However, with the help of *lepana* (a herbal concoction to see in darkness) that his master had given him, Andreux saw a magnificent tiger in what looked like a burrow under the mighty oak tree. The tree root hid most of the tiger from Andreux's view, but he could see the glimmer in the tiger's eyes from where he stood as it waited to pounce on its unsuspecting prey. Motionless, Andreux stared at the tiger, waiting for the right moment. A giant serpent on the top branches slithered uneasily. It had been many days since it had had a filling feast. Then Andreux saw Matunga, moving towards the predators. The deer moved an inch or two closer to the tiger, but not yet close enough.

The tiger and the snake waited patiently as the prey inched towards its death. Andreux knew he must act quickly.

He intentionally stepped on a twig and called, "Matunga!" The sound of the twig breaking and of Andreux's voice diverted the focus of the tiger. The deer jumped back. Not willing to lose its prey, the tiger leapt from its hiding place. Almost simultaneously the serpent dropped from the tree branches. However instead of falling on the deer, it fell on the tiger. The tiger hit the snake violently with its paws. The snake slithered around the waist of the beast and tightened its grip. The tiger fought back. As the snake squeezed and bit the tiger, the tiger tore at the snake with its claws and pinned it against a tree.

Andreux looked intently at the duel in front of him. He slowly walked backward with his eyes still fixed on the animals. He knew not to turn his back on them. Perhaps sensing that it was going to lose its prey, the tiger ripped the snake's head off and flung it away as he leapt towards Andreux, roaring hungrily. The dead snake's body slipped clumsily to the ground. Andreux was well prepared for the tiger, and he lifted his right arm and thrust his spear into the tiger's heart, killing it instantaneously.

He then picked up the deer in his strong arms and walked back to the tutelage of Hermitus, where he was studying. The tutelage was built on a small expanse of land that had been made available to Hermitus by Reganor, the deceased king of Vauns. It was located on the riverbank and was surrounded by forests on the remaining three sides. On the other side of the river was the Attymine Kingdom. The forest held abode to many magical and evil creatures, and therefore the only safe access to the tutelage was by river. The difficulty in access did not prevent the tutelage from being the most sought-after in its times.

The tutelage of Hermitus was not very large, but was famous. Disciples from beyond the Uldric Sea came to study there. Entry to the tutelage was protected to maintain the sanctity within the tutelage. Hermitus never taught for money; he had never had to pay his master and so he refused payment as well. Unlike so many other tutelages that now sprawled across the land, which charged anywhere from nine bulls to a yedib's supply of food grains to teach, his was absolutely free.

A tall fence built around the tutelage guarded it from the dangers of the forest. There were five cottages within the tutelage. Hermitus, the revered wizard, whose fame spread beyond mortal boundaries for his unsurpassed magical skills and fairness, lived in a cottage on the north corner, close to the forest. About forty disciples lived in the biggest cottage, located between the medic home and the kitchen. Hermitus taught his disciples in the fifth cottage.

Andreux approached a group of people standing outside the tutelage. He saw Mandrill, the gamekeeper, and he handed him the deer. The deer fed on grass and leaves to its heart's content, and Andreux rubbed its back with affection.

Hermitus looked at his most beloved deer and the young man petting it. "Well done, Andreux! I see that you have accomplished the task that you were assigned."

Andreux regarded the old man in front of him with respect. The past six hogashes of his master's life had done little to slow him down. Silver hair was the only clue to the true age of the robust man with astute intelligence.

"You would not have assigned me this task if you knew I would fail you," replied Andreux with humility. He could tell Hermitus was very pleased.

"Andreux! May the divine powers be with you for as long as you live. As a token of my appreciation, let me teach you a powerful spell that will help you when you are in grave danger."

Some of the disciples who were nearby spread the word that their master was teaching Andreux a new spell. As was custom, they gathered around the wizard and Andreux to observe. One of the disciples, Nevius, was upset when he heard this.

"It's not fair that master gives him chores and teaches him new spells because he completes them. Why don't the rest of us get the chance to learn new spells?" Nevius protested for all to hear.

"That's not true!" Andreux insisted. "You know, just as we all do, that Master does not give special treatment to anyone."

Hermitus turned towards Nevius. "Envy is not a good emotion to harbour, Nevius. It will corrupt your soul. The sooner you rid yourself of it, the better for yourself and for those around you. I have not taught this spell to anyone in a very long time—and for a very good reason. Not everyone is capable of learning it, let alone mastering it. I have chosen Andreux because I am confident he can withstand its power."

"I'm not finished saying what I want to say, Master!" said Nevius, raising his voice and advancing towards his master.

Andreux stepped forward to hold Nevius back, but Hermitus refrained Andreux from stepping in with a wave of his hand. The other disciples looked at Nevius in disbelief. Nobody had challenged the master before. Even Glimp, a fellow disciple, who literally worshipped the ground on which Nevius walked, stepped back.

"I warn you once again. But if you still think you are able, step forward and learn the spell." Hermitus pointed his wand to Nevius. Nevius took a step forward.

Andreux stepped aside. His eyes were fixed on the two, ready to absorb every detail of the proceedings. Nevius took a deep breath and remained focussed on his master's wand.

"When your life is in grave danger, say that you are surrounded by heavily armed enemies and you are unarmed, there is a spell that can come to your aid. It is called *Atmaitika*, or the self-empowerment spell. I have used this in the past to vanquish the 328 bandits who waylaid and surrounded the beautiful Queen Selvia. I have taught this spell to King Artheur, who used it to protect himself from the half-ogre Nogard. The spell is very powerful when used properly, and it does not require a wand. It involves willpower, confidence and concentration. Any slight hesitation on your part will yield deadly consequences, not to your enemies, but to you.

"Now Nevius, I want you to take a deep breath. You must stay calm and composed. I will try to attack you. While remaining focused, you must utter the spell three times and wave your right hand towards me, your opponent. Open your palm and roll the fingers while twisting your wrist, as if holding the end of a rope. Then thrust your right hand towards me as if you were throwing a lightning bolt at me. What you are doing in fact is repelling my moves and directing them back towards me. If you waver, you will not only not thwart my attempts, but you will also expose your weaknesses, which can be easily exploited by your opponents. Now come closer so that I can chant the spell in your ear."

Nevius moved closer to Hermitus, and Hermitus chanted the spell. Then Hermitus moved back. "Tell me when you are prepared. You may not get this chance in real life, so make the most of it," he said.

Nevius took a deep breath and tried to stay focussed. His right hand was ready to wave and his lips were busy chanting the spell. Andreux's eyes remained glued to the proceedings, and his mind was busy processing his master's instructions. Whether or not Nevius performed the spell correctly, Andreux was determined to master it.

Hermitus looked sharply at Nevius and waved his wand, uttering, "*Levitate-gravita oppo versuvia*[8]." Nevius waved his right hand and tried to catch the spell and throw it back at his master. But when he caught the spell, he felt its effect on him for a monnet. It lifted him off the ground and he hesitated. He quickly regained composure, but it was too late. He was floating in the air, as if suspended from an invisible latch. But that was just the effect of Hermitus's spell; when Nevius's *own* spell backfired, it exposed his weakness: his ego. An image, which looked exactly like him but was transparent, emerged from his body. The image faced Nevius and started to chant the Atmaitika spell that Hermitus had just taught him. And with each spell, Nevius was thrown higher and higher into the skies. Finally, after some time, when the power of the spell began to weaken, the image vanished. Nevius began to fall from high in the sky. He panicked when he realized that he was headed towards the rugged boulders. But he could do nothing to prevent it. The Atmaitika spell left him drained.

Just as Nevius was about to crash, Hermitus waved his wand. Nevius was left suspended above the piercing edge of a boulder. He was then transported back to where his master and his disciples were. When Hermitus waved his wand again, Nevius fainted and fell on the ground. Pompompulous and a few other disciples came forward and took him to the medic.

Hermitus addressed those disciples that remained at the scene. "Remember this experience and you will have learnt a valuable lesson. Nevius was not wrong in wanting to learn something new. In fact, I

---

8 Translates to 'Lift off the ground the opponent facing me'

admire his thirst for knowledge. But his motive was erroneous. He did not want knowledge to ward off evil forces. He wanted it in order to be superior to Andreux. As I mentioned before, envy is a very harmful emotion to harbour. We must all try to remove it from our hearts. Hopefully Nevius has learnt this lesson as well." Hermitus left his disciples and walked back to his chamber.

Having witnessed the incident, Andreux went looking for his mother, Arianne. She lived in the kitchen-cottage with the other staff. Andreux had spent his whole life in the tutelage, as had his cousin Senfred, unlike most of the other disciples who came from other cities and villages to study. When the two came of age to learn from Hermitus, they had moved from the kitchen-cottage to the disciples' cottage. Andreux and Senfred knew of little else outside the tutelage. Arianne had explained that Senfred's mother had died in childbirth and his father had left him in her custody when he had set out to fight some unknown enemy. She had told Andreux that his father had been a wealthy merchant but had died an unnatural death. The boys knew that they were refugees of some sort. Andreux assumed that was why his mother always wore a veil across her face in public. All that most people knew of her appearance was that she was tall for a woman and slender, with deep blue eyes. She, however, claimed that wearing the veil was their family tradition.

His mother, Aunt Arianne, as everyone called her, was a private person. She seldom talked with anyone. She was always busy helping with chores such as cooking, mending clothes, feeding the animals, upkeep of the library and so on. Her days were long and she rarely paused to rest. It almost seemed to Andreux as if she forced herself to be busy. Every day and every night, Andreux watched her thank the Almighty for showing them light at the end of the tunnel when all doors had seemed to close on them simultaneously. Andreux had many questions about his past, but she never really answered them. Senfred, it seemed, never had so many questions.

Senfred had once attempted to explain his reasoning to Andreux. They had been plucking vegetables from the kitchen garden and Senfred had said, "What has happened in my past has happened. If I'm destined to know it, I'm sure I will sooner or later. I'm content the way I am. I'm glad to have you and Aunt Arianne in my life, and that's all that matters." Andreux had been taken aback. His cousin, his best friend, had become a young man at peace with himself and the world. Inside the vibrant, athletic and lean stature lay an inner calm that remained beyond Andreux's reach.

Andreux admired Senfred for many things. Senfred was always frank about his opinion. He never tried to sweeten his words about his emotions towards various things and people. Senfred would analyze the two sides of an argument and stick with what he perceived to be right.

Whenever Andreux and Senfred had an argument, they would go to Arianne, who would always diffuse it by saying that healthy arguments strengthen true friendship and that they should be able to work out their differences.

Andreux found his mother helping the medic in attending to Nevius, who was regaining consciousness. When she spotted Andreux, she walked towards him and gave him a warm embrace. They walked out of the cottage.

"I understand that you have saved the master's deer. You cannot imagine how proud you have made me today. Your father ..." she stopped in mid-sentence and her eyes filled with tears. Andreux was surprised by the rare reference to his father.

"What about my father? Tell me, Mother, and don't dodge the questions like you usually do." He smiled to soften the harshness in his words.

"I won't, my child. I just wanted to say your father would have been so proud of you today. If only he were alive." She wiped her tears.

"You never told me how he died," said Andreux.

"I wish I had an answer for you. All I know is he was killed. I have yet to see his ..." Andreux could tell she was fighting hard to remain composed. "I never saw his dead body."

But Andreux couldn't let it go. He needed answers. "Then how do you know that he was killed? Who killed him?"

"I'm sorry Andreux, but I can't bear to relive those moments in my life. I will promise you one thing. Not very long from now, all your questions will be answered. The time is almost here. But for now I want you to focus on your studies." With that she left him standing there, full of unanswered questions.

Senfred joined his cousin as Arianne walked away. "She's fighting many demons from her past, Andreux," he said.

"I know. I wish I could help. I wish she would let me in."

"She said the time is almost here, didn't she? Let us give her some more time."

"I don't have a choice, do I?" said Andreux, and he decided to drop the topic.

Later that afternoon, Pompompulous joined them. He was oldest among the disciples. Andreux and Senfred became friends with him easily. They could converse without worrying about the age gap. Moreover, Andreux and Senfred would shower him with questions about life beyond the tutelage. His answers fascinated them. He was their cherished source of worldly wisdom.

Andreux was in awe when Pompompulous told them that his father had once been thrown into prison because he had had the courage to speak against the king. "My father has always told me to be honest and truthful about who I am and what I believe in. And when I give my word, it's for life," Pompompulous had explained.

The friends spent quite some time discussing the various potions that their master had taught them the day before. As it started to get dark, Andreux remembered that he needed to look up some old documents in the library. "I need to look up the herbimedic to study the remedies for snake venom," he told Senfred and Pompompulous as he left.

He was walking past his master's chamber when he heard his mother's voice. He slowed his pace, not intending to eavesdrop, but when he found that he could hear her words clearly, he stopped to listen.

"I have never for a moment forgotten my past, and that has helped me to maintain my focus on the future I am planning for them. Andreux is growing fast and his questions only seem to be increasing ..."

"It is only youthful inquisitiveness, my child!"

"I understand. But I'm not sure I can keep this secret to myself any longer. I truly hope that I hear from Veritus soon."

"I am sure he is on his way to give us the news."

Andreux heard footsteps walking towards the chamber door, so he hurried on towards the library. He was filled with apprehension and excitement. The secret that his mother had guarded for the past one and one-half hogashes would be revealed to him very soon. *I wonder who Veritus is!* he thought to himself.

Chapter Two
Nevius, son of Nebulus

The path to salvation is not always straight.
Strayed if you, come back before it's too late.
Once you've made up your mind, walked through the gate,
the only way out is what's locked in your fate.

Nevius was filled with hatred towards Andreux and contempt towards
Hermitus. He wanted revenge for the humiliation that he had suffered
in front of his friends. He came from a very rich family that showed no
mercy to the downtrodden. He had servants and slaves who attended
to all his needs. He had not however, been admitted to the tutelage
because of his family's wealth. Hermitus said that he had noticed
Nevius's intelligence, which showed hope of a bright future. Nevius
knew that his father was widely believed to be the chief supporter of
Nefarius, the present ruler of Vauns. He also suspected that Hermitus,
who was known to be impartial and non-partisan, took an exception
with Nefarius.

Nevius's animosity to Andreux came naturally. Andreux was
everyone's pet. He set the examples for everyone else. Andreux could
do nothing wrong. It was exactly the opposite for Nevius. Right from
the start, it was obvious that whatever he did was below his master's
expectations. In fact, he was becoming the example of what *not* to do.
And he did not try to prove himself, because he never had to try thus
far. So as any other average human being would do (although Nevius
strongly objected to being called average), he looked around him, and
not within, for the cause of his unhappiness, and he had concluded
that it was Andreux. Thus the feud began.

Nevius built his own team of followers. His status in society, or
rather his father's, made the task easy. There were quite a few who
would have gladly given up everything just to stand next to him.
Nevius developed his group with complete recklessness. He gave them

silver coins and gifts, promised them better lives once they moved out of the tutelage and threatened those who questioned him with severe punishment from the king himself. He called them names and teased them often. That did not deter the others from wanting to hang out with him.

Glimp was one of his chief admirers. He washed Nevius's clothes and made his bed. He saved portions of his food to share with Nevius. Though Nevius continuously complained about how dirty his clothes were or how rumpled his bed was and argued that he never ate Glimp's food portions, Glimp remained steadfast in his devotion. Nevius knew that he was Glimp's only hope of rising from abject poverty and stepping up the social ladder. But Nevius would throw him away, as he would pieces of shredded rags, once he was no longer useful to him.

After Hermitus almost got Nevius killed with Atmaitika, as Nevius explained it to his followers, it became his goal in life to seek revenge. Had Hermitus not chosen Andreux to teach Atmaitika, Nevius would not have objected in the first place. Andreux had everything to do with it. And therefore Nevius had to seek revenge on Andreux.

A few days later, after the Atmaitika incident, Hermitus gathered all his disciples to teach them the effects of various types of snake venom and antidotes for each type. To make the class more interesting, he even brought several snakes, which were all kept secure in glass cages. The presence of live snakes in the class caused a variety of reactions from the disciples. Nevius sniggered when Pompompulous shrieked at the sight of them and refused to attend the class. However, as Pompompulous was not allowed to miss the class, he remained as far as possible from the cages.

Nevius's smile disappeared when he noticed that Andreux and Senfred were interested in learning about snakes. Vengeance clouded his mind as he plotted a diabolical scheme. Nevius wanted to learn as much as possible and so remained at the front of the gathering as well. Glimp was next to him, though Nevius knew he wished he had stayed behind Pompompulous.

Hermitus opened the glass lid and picked up a green cobra with brown patches.

"This is the Negi snake, which, because of its body texture and colour, can very easily hide among branches and shrubs. It is a rare breed of snake but is quite commonly found in the nearby forests. Its poison has no effect on any part of the body other than the brain. If a bite from the Negi were not treated in time, its victim would be brain dead."

Hermitus then slid the snake back into the cage before he secured the lid once more. He then picked up a small bottle and a branch with oval-shaped leaves. "This is the antidote for the Negi poison. It is an herb, called *life-petal*, also commonly found in Aranya. More than the herb itself, it is the timing of administering the antidote that fights the poison." He continued, "The antidote has to be taken within twelve monnets. The poison spreads to the brain through the blood system in about twelve monnets and therefore it is paramount for the victim to have the antidote within that time. The antidote, when taken, goes straight to the brain and protects it from the poison."

Hermitus then moved to the next cage and pulled out another snake, which was black with white spots on its body. Nevius thought it looked like a miniature version of a dark sky filled with stars.

"This is the dark-slider. This snake's venom has a curious effect on its victims. It does not kill them. It will, however, cause them to behave contrary to their usual disposition. The poison's effect will wear down in less than a day, without the need for any antidote."

Nevius vigorously took detailed notes of everything that Hermitus talked about in class.

When Hermitus finally declared the class over, he had discussed twelve different snakes, their venoms and antidotes. Having noticed Nevius's thorough note-taking during the class, Hermitus approached him. "I must say that I am pleasantly surprised to see your interest in the subject matter. After all, you have found something that interests you. That is a beginning."

Nevius merely nodded. Hermitus was right about that. It was a beginning, just not the beginning he expected.

Everyone left the room, talking animatedly. Some were frightened, whereas others were excited to have learnt about snake venom. Glimp was sweating profusely and could barely speak.

"That was an exciting class, wasn't it!" exclaimed Nevius as he walked towards Glimp. He knew that Glimp loathed snakes, but that did not stop him. He pulled out a parchment from his bag and thrust it into Glimp's hands.

"Look at this snake," he said as Glimp hesitated to hold the parchment in his hand. "Negi, the deadly cobra is found right here in Aranya. Do you know what it means?"

His friend shook his head.

"It's the moment I've been waiting for. All I need is some venom from Negi. I'll use it to poison Andreux, somewhere he won't be able to get the antidote on time. And I'll finally win!" His eyes gleamed with sadistic pleasure as he uttered these words.

Glimp appeared to be taken aback at this sudden announcement.

"Talking about revenge is all right. Making detailed plans to actually kill someone is different," murmured Glimp. Nevius was surprised to hear another voice come from within Glimp at that very moment. "I never thought you hated Andreux enough to kill him." The voice was cold and calculating, very unlike Glimp.

"Are you trying to tell me what to do? You have done things in the past that I can easily expose if you ever betray me. I'm your only chance of making it in this life. So keep your opinions to yourself and help me when I need it." Nevius knew his words had the intended impact when Glimp's face turned ash white.

A few days later, Nevius found out that Hermitus was finally going to teach Andreux Atmaitika. It was the day Andreux was turning one and one-half hogashes. He summoned Andreux to the open fields. When Nevius reached the open fields to witness the teaching, he found several other disciples gathered there.

Hermitus pointed his wand to Andreux. "Do you remember everything that I told Nevius the other day, when I taught him Atmaitika?" Andreux nodded. His eyes were fixed on the master's wand. Nevius waited with anticipation and remained focused on the proceedings.

"Then come closer so that I can chant the spell in your ear." Hermitus chanted the spell and moved back. Andreux took a deep breath and Nevius could tell he remained calm and focused. His right hand was ready to wave and his lips were busy chanting the spell.

Hermitus waved his wand uttering "*Levitate-gravita oppo versuvia.*" Andreux waved his right hand, caught the spell and threw it back at his master.

While Andreux was returning the spell, Nevius stomped on Glimp's right foot. Glimp would have kept quiet under normal circumstances, however, he heard the strange, calculating voice again; this time it spoke only to him.

Shout now. Andreux will lose focus and no one will blame you. Glimp was astonished at his own thoughts. He was captivated by the words and without any further thought, shouted in pain. Andreux was distracted by Glimp's cry. As soon as he lost focus, the spell, which had not yet reached Hermitus, came back and hit Andreux with its full power. Andreux, who quickly regained his composure, withstood the spell when it hit him. However, the spell was too powerful, and he was surrounded by translucent figures that shouted at him, "You have no father, you have no father." Andreux closed his ears and fell to the ground, defenceless. A smile escaped Nevius's lips. He now knew Andreux's weakness.

Hermitus quickly retracted the spell and the figures disappeared. He walked to Andreux, who was getting up from the ground.

"Are you all right, Andreux?" he asked.

"I think I am. I should not have lost my focus," replied Andreux.

"It happens to the best of us when we learn the first time. You have withstood its power without causing much damage to yourself. Would you like to try it again?" he asked.

Andreux stood up and bowed to Hermitus. He then took a deep breath and nodded.

Hermitus cast the spell again. Andreux countered it with Atmaitika. Nevius tried to distract him, but his attempts were foiled when Senfred and Pompompulous grabbed him by his arms and dragged him away from the scene. Glimp tried feebly to stop them, but he could not match up to Andreux's friends. He fell back on the ground, when Pompompulous pushed him away. As he was getting up, he heard the voice one more time.

You are such a loser. Glimp looked up and saw a transparent image standing in front of him, staring him in the eye. Glimp's voice was choked with fear. He could barely utter a word.

The image was no different than Glimp himself, except it was just an image, not a human being of flesh and blood. The eyes of the image were angry, like tiny balls of fire. The face held a look of contempt.

Quick. Get back on your feet fast. The image's voice was authoritative and held Glimp its captive. Glimp got up and lifted his head up slowly to look at the image.

"Who are you?" he managed to whimper.

You can call me Gruber. I will be your friend and guide from this monnet. In turn you will let me stay in you. Together we will achieve what you have not dared to dream. Replied the image.

"Are you a ghost?" Glimp was very scared, his face was ash-white.

No I am not. I am your alter-ego. I represent all that you desired deep within. You may call me your inner voice. Sniggered Gruber. Glimp gave in meekly without any further questions. He was afraid, yet he was secretly excited about what just happened. While being held back, Nevius watched as Andreux repelled the master's spell successfully. Nevius saw Hermitus patting Andreux on the shoulder as Senfred and Pompompulous dragged Nevius back to their master.

"We caught Nevius trying to sabotage your lesson, Master."

"Is that true, Nevius?".

Nevius held his head high but remained silent.

"I warned you earlier not to harbour envy, but it appears that you have not understood. Listen carefully, once and for all. Get rid of envy, before it gets the better of you. This is your second warning. There will not be a next time."

Nevius remained unperturbed on the surface, but his blood boiled with rage.

He made a slight change in his plans to get rid of Andreux. He decided to administer the green cobra's poison to Andreux that very night, just before he went to sleep. He would also make sure Andreux slept through the ordeal, so that he would not wake up or wake others who might spoil his plan. He would get close to Andreux by apologizing to him. Once Andreux forgave him, which Nevius was almost certain of, the rest would be easy. But first he had to find the green cobra.

He looked for it everywhere. First he searched the tutelage to find out where his master kept the caged snakes. When he asked Mandrill, the animal keeper as to their whereabouts, the skinny old man told him that the master had caged them only for the lesson. They had all been released from their cages as soon as the session was done. That news dampened Nevius's spirits. He was hoping not to spend too much time looking for the snake. He knew that much of the time he had before nightfall needed to be spent in gaining Andreux's trust.

He rushed out of the tutelage like a tornado, knocking down several things that came in his way: a lamp, a broom and the disciple using it, a squash-vine and Pompompulous, to name a few. Pompompulous lost his balance and fell in the animal barn. This resulted in a spectacular commotion, with birds flying everywhere and animals running here and there.

Nevius did not stay around to help restore the peace. Instead, he went off in search of the cobra, though he did not wander far into the forest. He was afraid to test uncharted waters, and his enmity with Andreux came a close second to his own well-being. He looked around to see if he could spot the snake. He remembered that it camouflaged itself among branches and shrubs. He also remembered that it fed on small birds. He quickly ran back out of the forest, straight to the animal farm and stole a little duckling. The pandemonium in the barn had not yet settled down by then, which he believed would ensure that no one saw him enter or leave.

He went back to the forest with the prey. He selected a spot that he thought would be the most likely place to find the cobra and held the bird in his hand. The duckling quacked in fear, and before long the cobra appeared in sight. As soon as Nevius saw the snake, he let go of the bird and took out his knife. The bird escaped in terror and was never seen again. The reptile slithered menacingly towards him, with a loud hissing sound. Nevius threw the net he held in his other hand over the cobra. While the snake tried to escape from the net, Nevius attacked it with his knife repeatedly. The snake tried to bite him, but Nevius was surprisingly quick and agile. Very soon the snake died, unable to withstand the wounds inflicted by the merciless knife. Nevius carefully milked the snake's venom glands and poured the poison in a small container that he had in his robe pocket. He then closed the container tightly and put it back in his pocket.

He was about to leave when he heard an explosion behind him. When he looked back, he saw the dead body of the snake going up in fumes. In its place a dark figure emerged. It was hard to tell if it was a man or a woman. It was covered in tattered robes and stood tall, hovering above Nevius, who looked like a pygmy beside it. For a face, it had a swarm of bees, which left gaps in between for eyes, nose and mouth. Nevius felt his stomach tie up in knots when he saw the creature's face. When the creature spoke, it was an eerie hissing whisper that Nevius heard. He felt a cold chill climbing up his spine and he shivered. *This must be the half-world creature that master always cautioned us about at the tutelage,* he thought. His mind was trying to recollect if there was anyway he could get away from this deadly encounter, but he drew a blank.

"You thought you could get away with killing the snake, you little good-for-nothing?"

"I'm sorry. I didn't know," Nevius whimpered.

"You don't get away with such pathetic excuses with me. You have to pay the price for killing my trusted aide." The hissing was becoming unbearable. The creature inched closer to him. It stank of a decomposed body, which sent Nevius's head reeling.

"Like I said, I'm sorry. I'll do whatever you want me to. Please let me go," Nevius pleaded.

"Too late for that. You have to live with the consequences of your action. Welcome to the half-world," it said as it bent down to kiss him.

Nevius could not offer any resistance, though his inner resolve was revolting from within. He collapsed as the bees stung him all over his face.

When he woke up, the creature was nowhere to be found. He felt weak and defenceless, but that was all. He searched his pocket for the poison container and found it safe and secure. He felt relieved. He walked back to the tutelage.

He saw Glimp waiting nervously at the tutelage gate that was about to be closed off at dusk, and waved to him. When he approached him, however, Glimp screamed. Nevius did not understand why he was screaming until Glimp took him to the pond and showed Nevius his reflection in the water. Nevius was aghast. His face was decomposing. His eyes were shrinking into the sockets, which seemed large and empty. The skin on his face was peeling off slowly, showing the skull beneath. Glimp ran away from Nevius, screaming for his life. Nevius sat there next to the pond like an uprooted tree.

The news about Nevius spread like wildfire and soon Hermitus came to him. Almost the entire tutelage came with him. Everyone else stopped at a distance. Nevius covered his face with his hands, so that no one could see him. When Hermitus came closer, he pulled his hands away to see him. Nevius could tell that he was taken aback for a quick moment.

"I feel sorry for you, young man. What have you done to deserve the wrath of half-world?" he asked. Nevius could not answer him. Instead, he started to cry uncontrollably. Hermitus did not stop him. When Nevius's sobs subdued, he asked him again. "You must have done something to have this happen to you. Confide and I will know the exact cure for you. It's time to come clean," he said.

Nevius was in a dilemma. If he told the entire truth, Hermitus would expel him for trying to kill Andreux. But if he didn't tell, he may have to live like a leper all his life.

"Well, Master, I was in the forest trying to learn more about the snakes, when a green cobra attacked me. I killed it in an attempt to save myself, when it turned into a dark-hooded horrible creature. Its face was covered with bees. I fainted when it kissed me. When I woke up, my face was all distorted and decomposing. That was all, Master," he said, hiding his face with his hands.

Hermitus shook his head with disbelief. "Are you sure there is nothing else to tell me?" he asked.

"Nothing else, Master," said Nevius. His voice clearly lacked conviction, his words were barely audible.

"Then I am afraid, there is nothing I can help you with," he said.

"I don't understand. I told you everything," said Nevius.

"You are a fool to continue lying to me. Did you know that a Negi does not attack humans? And if it was a creature from half-world as you were describing it to be, then it would not approach you unless you had offered it an excuse to do so, such as attacking it without provocation or snatching away its food. Therefore I am asking you for the final time, what have you done to deserve this, O Nevius, son of Nebulus?" Hermitus almost shouted.

Everyone who gathered there fell silent. Everyone except Mandrill. "Master, if I may interrupt."

"What is it, Mandrill?" asked Hermitus.

"Some time earlier, Nevius came to the animal farm looking for the snakes that you brought to the class a few days earlier. Later, he ran off like a gust of wind to the forest, toppling everything that came in his way. And while we were busy cleaning up his mess, he came back to steal a duckling."

"He must have taken it to lure the cobra," Senfred thought out aloud.

"to get the snake venom ..." Andreux paused.

"You wanted to get cobra venom to kill Andreux, didn't you?" Pompompulous shouted angrily.

There it was; his scheme was out in the open, for everyone to see.

"Is it true what I hear, Nevius?" asked Hermitus. Nevius had no choice now that his scheme was given away. He nodded and fell on his master's feet in fear. Hermitus stepped back.

"For the crime that you had planned to commit, there is no forgiveness. The fact that you did not succeed is not a valid reason to excuse you. You have shown time and again that you cannot be trusted. I will restore your face, but you are herewith expelled from my tutelage. If I see you again in my tutelage, I will not think twice about feeding you to the creatures of the half-world myself." Hermitus waved his wand and chanted a spell. Nevius's face returned back to its normal self.

Nevius was relieved that he no longer looked like a leper, but Andreux had once again succeeded, this time in getting him kicked out of the tutelage. He immediately packed his clothes, books, knives, and darts and left. But he did not go far because he was afraid of running into the half-world creatures again. He found a cave near the riverbed, but found huge footprints and bones with raw meat stuck to them and decided to stay away from that as well. He did not return to his home yet. He wanted to finish what he had started. He found a dilapidated dwelling far from the tutelage, in a clearing near the forest. He set up his temporary home there.

He still had his cobra poison with him, and he still had his darts. Now all he needed was Andreux to come within shooting distance. He was in no hurry. He decided to wait patiently for the right opportunity.

Strange sightings in tutelage, spoken and seen
lead to a dangerous quest for minds that are keen.
Harmed are the innocent lives caught in between,
by evil that roams free in the forest, unseen.

Andreux, on his way to the grounds the next day, found Glimp huddled in a corner, talking to himself in a hushed voice. He was sitting next to the bed that had previously been occupied by Nevius. *He must be missing Nevius,* he thought. As Andreux approached him, Glimp became quiet.

"Were you talking about me?" asked Andreux, "Or something that matters to me? Why did you become quiet when you saw me?"

"It was nothing of that sort, actually." Glimp appeared to be covering up, and Andreux was not convinced.

"Come on. Now that Nevius is gone, you don't have to be afraid of him. I know you. You were fun to be around before he showed up at the tutelage. Why don't you take this opportunity to start fresh?"

"But we weren't talking about Nevius. I was just saying that …" Glimp stopped in mid-sentence, and his alter ego, Gruber, finished it for him. "He was just saying that we had seen a stranger roaming outside the tutelage near the forest."

Andreux looked around, "Who is the 'we' that you are referring to? I don't see anyone here."

"That is beside the point. The issue is that someone is roaming outside the tutelage and it is not good for any of us," Gruber reiterated. Glimp meekly gave in to Gruber.

"Are you serious?" asked Andreux.

"Yes! I totally forgot about it yesterday, with what happened to Nevius."

"If it's true, we need to bring this to Master's attention right away. It could be a serious matter," said Andreux.

Glimp dragged his feet the whole way. On their way, they ran into Pompompulous and Senfred.

"What has he done now? With Nevius gone, I figured he would've mellowed out," Pompompulous said, looking suspiciously at Glimp, who was hiding behind Andreux.

"Actually *they* made an important observation," said Andreux reassuringly. When Pompompulous looked around, Andreux could not help but burst out in laughter. Then he paused, expecting Glimp to tell Pompompulous what he'd seen. However, Glimp was strangely quiet.

After an awkward moment, Andreux spoke up. "He has seen a stranger roaming outside the tutelage."

"Then I wasn't hallucinating!" said Pompompulous, his voice squeaking in excitement.

"What do you mean? Did you see him too?"

"I wasn't sure last night, but it makes sense. I also saw a stranger yesterday. I was returning from the forest to report it when Nevius bumped into me. Again last night, I thought I saw someone leave the tutelage, but I couldn't see the stranger's face. I was actually coming to you now to discuss it," said Pompompulous.

Andreux noticed that Glimp eased up when he heard this. He smiled a little. "Is it possible that Nevius is somehow still in the tutelage? Is that who you are mistaking for a stranger in the dark?" Andreux suggested. *But why would Nevius risk coming back the same night he had been kicked out? Also, what about the stranger in the woods? Obviously that could not have been Nevius.*

"May I make a suggestion?" said Senfred. "The only way we can solve this mystery is to go to where Pompompulous saw—or thought he saw—the stranger."

"I don't know if that's such a good idea." Pompompulous frowned. "If it was Nevius, then he would be ready to attack Andreux again. I don't want to do anything that might harm you."

"I'm not afraid of Nevius, and I'll watch out for him," said Andreux. "As long as I'm with my friends, I'll be safe. I think we should go and investigate."

Pompompulous agreed to join Andreux and Senfred in their quest. They decided not to inform the master of their secret mission just yet. Glimp decided to stay back in the tutelage.

Andreux, Senfred and Pompompulous walked through the gates of tutelage and headed towards the riverbed where Pompompulous thought he had seen the stranger entering the forest.

As they neared the riverbed, Senfred exclaimed, "Look over here!"

There were muddy footprints that made a trail leading towards the forest. They appeared new. It could have been anyone from the tutelage, but they had not seen anyone go that way. With increasing excitement, they followed the footprints. Andreux noticed that the footprints were not even, the left footprint was deeper than the right one. Apparently the person who made those prints did not walk steadily. While attempting to trace the footprints, the friends reached a cave that was practically hidden from view until they approached it.

Andreux noted that the cave was small and its entrance was almost covered by the huge tree that grew in front of it. The footprints stopped abruptly at the entrance. Andreux watched as Pompompulous looked all around, but could not figure out where the person could have gone from there. Andreux looked into the cave to find out if humans or animals occupied it. He found some twigs on the ground that had been burning for some time and had recently been put out. He also found some morsels of food near the extinguished fire. Someone was living in the cave!

They searched the cave for more clues but could find none. They went back to the cave entrance and checked the footprints again. They went around the tree in a circle. They looked up the tree to see if someone was hiding, but they found no one.

"One thing is clear. Pompompulous did actually see someone here," said Andreux.

"But who is it and what is the person doing in this cave?" asked Senfred. None of them had any answers. After a brief discussion, the friends decided to split up and look for more clues in different directions. They all agreed to return to the cave entrance shortly.

Andreux went looking behind the cave to see if there was a path leading into or out of the cave. He found none. He also looked for other signs of human habitation, but he found none of these either. As he came out of the cave, he watched Senfred climbing the tree in front of the cave to spot any movement in the vicinity. Senfred waited there for some time before he climbed down. Pompompulous searched in front of the cave and a little beyond.

After a half hour, they met to discuss their findings.

"Could someone be watching us without our knowledge?" said Andreux.

"We've checked every path to this cave and found no one. That isn't possible," said Senfred.

Pompompulous sighed. "But I followed the footprints until they stopped abruptly—they seemed to disappear or perhaps they were erased. How do you explain that?"

"That I don't know. We can hide behind the tree and watch," said Senfred.

So they all hid behind the tree and waited. Soon it started to get dark, and Pompompulous suggested that they return to tutelage. As they were walking back, Senfred signalled to the other two to be quiet. He whispered that he thought he heard someone walking. They waited for some time, but they heard nothing else. Andreux thought this whole stranger mystery might be nothing, but he decided to come back tomorrow to investigate anyway.

When the three friends returned to the tutelage, Andreux found his mother waiting anxiously for them.

"Where have you been? I was beginning to get worried," she said.

"We were just walking near the riverbed. Nothing of any consequence," replied Andreux.

Seeing that they were all safe and sound, Arianne returned to her chores.

Later that night, Andreux and Senfred talked about Nevius.

"I need to find out tomorrow if he's still hiding in the forest," said Andreux.

"I don't want you to become obsessed with that idea," Senfred replied.

"That's easy for you to say. It's my life that's on the line. I have every right to make sure that Nevius is gone for good," said Andreux vehemently.

"But you must remember that nothing should be done without our master's knowledge or approval."

Just then Pompompulous joined them. He appeared to be out of breath. "Guess what I just found out!" he said loudly.

Andreux motioned him to lower his voice lest he attract anyone's attention.

Pompompulous continued in a hushed tone. "I overheard Glimp talking to himself a little while ago. Apparently, Nevius is still roaming in the forest, so it wasn't a stranger that he saw," he said animatedly.

"Glimp must be losing his mind, I caught him talking to himself this morning. He keeps referring to himself as 'we' and 'he,' as if he were not one but two people," said Andreux.

"Well at least his gibberish confirms our suspicion that the stranger in the forest is Nevius," said Senfred.

"But that isn't possible," said Pompompulous. "As I was looking for you, I saw the stranger. It's definitely not Nevius. As soon as I saw him, I came running to alert you," he said.

"Where is he now?" asked Andreux.

"Near Master's chamber."

Andreux ran in that direction. But the stranger appeared to notice that he was being followed, so he quickened his pace. After a few quick steps, the stranger turned around to see how much distance separated them, and Andreux caught a glimpse of his face.

Though the features were marred by darkness, Andreux was certain that it was a man. He had a thick moustache and beard? While Andreux tried to get a closer look, the man slipped back into the shadows and disappeared. Andreux continued to run after him but did not find him.

When he returned, Senfred and Pompompulous were full of questions.

"Did you catch the stranger?"

"Did you see the face?"

"Was it Nevius?"

"Was it a man or a woman?"

"Which way did the person go?"

"It was a man, but it wasn't Nevius. In fact he's not anyone that we've seen before. He raced into the darkness and was gone in a moment. There must be a secret hiding place somewhere there," replied Andreux. "We must look again tomorrow."

The next day was mostly uneventful. They did not find any new clues as to the whereabouts of the stranger, neither in the tutelage where Andreux had lost him the night before, nor at the cave. In fact, the cave had been cleaned up. The footprints were gone, and so were the burnt twigs.

"Someone knew we were here looking for them. They've cleaned up their act and left. I don't think we'll find them here again," said Senfred, looking dismayed.

Andreux was disappointed as well. Last night he had been so close to catching the stranger, yet he could not do so. They walked back to tutelage.

"Do you see that?" said Andreux, pointing to the cave. Not very far from it, there were signs of someone or something being dragged through the dried leaves and branches on the ground. The three friends followed the trail further into the forest. Andreux looked around constantly for any suspicious movements behind them.

At the end of the trail, to their horror, they found a man collapsed under a tree. He was lying on the ground facedown. When Senfred turned the man over, he exclaimed, "It's Mandrill!"

Just then Andreux saw a figure recede behind the trees. It was becoming quite dark in the forest, so Andreux took his torch with him to see who it was.

"Wait for me, Andreux," said Senfred. "Pompompulous, look after Mandrill, and I'll go with Andreux." As Andreux and Senfred followed the figure, Andreux noticed that the figure wore dark robes and its face was hidden under a hood. It seemed to float in the air, making it difficult to follow. Then it disappeared with a hiss as the friends approached it.

"It's getting dark. We need to go back," said Senfred. Though Andreux wanted to pursue the creature, he knew that Mandrill needed care. So they returned to Pompompulous and then to the tutelage, carrying Mandrill with them. They rushed him to the medic and informed Hermitus of what happened. Andreux stayed back to help his mother.

Mandrill recovered in a few hours. Andreux was still around when Mandrill told Hermitus what had happened. "Earlier today, I saw Andreux, Senfred and Pompompulous go into the woods."

Andreux shifted uneasily at this mention.

"The frequency with which they have been visiting the forest was increasing and I became curious. I wanted to find out what they were doing, so I left the animal farm in the care of Glimp and followed Andreux and the other two. At one point I thought I saw Nevius. But he was not following anyone. In fact he was running as if someone was chasing him. Then I saw another man, whom I did not recognize, running after Nevius. When I returned to my search for Andreux and the others, I did not find them. But what I did find was a half-world creature. The creature told me that I had trespassed into its territory. When I objected to its accusation, it laughed with a terrible hiss and said 'Gone are the days when we abided by your rules. The forest is ours and anyone coming in shall do so at their own risk.' The creature then grabbed me with its skeletal hands and kissed me, sucking out my life. I fell to the ground, trying to resist. As I fell, I saw a bright light coming in my direction, and that caused the creature to run away. The next thing I remember is waking up at the medic's."

Andreux was remorseful when he heard Mandrill. He realized that his curiosity had put other lives in danger. In the future, he would have to exercise caution while acting on his impulses, he told himself.

Arianne and Hermitus attended to Mandrill all night. Later that night, Andreux walked to the master's chamber to enquire about Mandrill, when to his astonishment, he saw the stranger step out of the chamber and disappear into the shadows. Not wanting to upset his master by showing up at his doorstep at an awkward time, he returned to his bed. Yet he could not sleep until almost the early hours of morning.

When he woke up the next morning, it was unusually late. In fact, had Glimp not woken him up, he might have slept in a little longer. He woke Andreux to tell him the master had a very important announcement to make. Andreux got ready in a hurry and dashed out to hear the announcement.

Hermitus was standing at the entrance of his chamber. Everyone was gathered in front of him, looking at him eagerly, waiting for his announcement. Andreux heard some of them speculating that it had to do with whatever happened to Mandrill. Some feared that Mandrill had died from the attack and were mentally preparing themselves to mourn for him. Andreux stood next to Senfred, feeling guilt-ridden. If it were not for them, the half-world creature would not have attacked Mandrill.

Hermitus cleared his throat. "I have some good news and bad news. The good news is that Mandrill will recover. The bad news is that danger is lurking around in the most unexpected corners of the forest. As such, no one is allowed to step out of the tutelage boundaries at any time, day or night. Anyone doing so will be immediately expelled from the tutelage for reckless behaviour. I will fight the evil forces that roam beyond the tutelage boundaries and will keep you informed of my progress."

After the announcement was complete, the gates were closed. Torches were lit along the boundary walls in order to reveal any creature that might try to sneak into the tutelage.

For the next eight days, the disciples were busy with their studies. Andreux had no free time at all. He thought about the face in the dark whenever he had a moment to catch a breath of fresh air. When he talked about this with Senfred, Senfred advised him not to put his or other people's lives in danger. Andreux mentioned seeing the stranger step out of the master's chamber. He did not want any more trouble because of their secret mission. They decided to wait until their master lifted the ban from stepping outside the tutelage.

But the problems only seemed to multiply. The cook announced that food and utensils were being stolen from the kitchen. Andreux was assigned the duty of monitoring kitchen supplies. That afternoon, he and Senfred were summoned by Hermitus.

"I need you to look up some old parchments in the library for me," he said.

"What type of parchments, Master?" enquired Andreux.

"They are in the attic, in an old wooden box that has been sealed for a long time now. It may take both of you to break the lock open. Once the box is open, you will find that the parchments are sorted into three bundles. Fetch me the cloth bundle with a red shield painted on it."

Andreux and Senfred brought the box down from the attic. The box had not been touched for many yedibs and dust had settled on it in thick layers. The friends brushed the dust off and broke the lock. Andreux found the bundle that his master was looking for. The words *Duell dragonisla*[9] were written on the shield.

Hermitus smiled as he held it in his hands. "Still as new as it was two hogashes ago," he said, taking pride in his possession. "And as relevant as ever."

Andreux watched as Hermitus opened the bundle, and he noticed that the scriptures had faded with time. "May I help you with finding any particular parchment?"

"Certainly!" said Hermitus. "In fact, I want you to read them all and make detailed notes. I might ask you for some of your notes when I require them. These were compiled by my master, and I have only had to use one parchment in all these hogashes."

Andreux was thrilled to be involved in his master's fight against half-world creatures. He and Senfred spent a lot of time going through the ancient scriptures.

Between kitchen supervision, his own studies, and helping the master go through old parchments to help him fight the half-world creatures, Andreux barely managed time to catch a nap at night. Every day, he helped Hermitus until sundown. He would then proceed to the kitchen to supervise supper preparations. This continued for the next eight days.

On the ninth day, there was a change in plans for Andreux. The kitchen matron called for him as soon as he woke up. Suspecting another theft, Andreux met her immediately. However, she had some good news for him.

"As there has been no stealing of food or utensils reported for the past few days, you are now off kitchen supervision," she told him.

9 *Duell dragonisla* is translated as "Duel the demons."

Andreux was relieved; that would give him more time to pursue the stranger's whereabouts. Later in the afternoon, Hermitus called for him.

"With your help, I have figured out a way to fight the half-world creatures. As a result, we no longer need to go through the parchments," he informed Andreux.

Though this meant more time for Andreux, he wanted to participate in the fight against the half-world creatures. "Master, may I go with you while you fight the evil forces?" he asked.

"Why didn't I think of that? You need not be a bystander anymore, as you are now of proper age to take part in the proceedings. Exercise caution, precision of timing and judgement."

Andreux found his master's words encouraging. He followed his master to his chamber. Hermitus locked the chamber for most of the day and ordered that no one disturb them.

Andreux helped Hermitus stack up the spell-parchments in sequence and draw circles and other patterns in each corner of the chamber. Hermitus waved his right hand at the main wall in his chamber and uttered:

"*Drusyo mana vanchitvo!*[10]"

The wall became transparent and an image appeared on it. Andreux recognized it at once. "It is Aranya," he said enthusiastically.

"Very good. We are going to use this to locate all the half-world creatures that are hiding in it," said Hermitus.

Andreux pulled out the relevant parchments. "For that you will need *Indictora*, the spell to locate, then *Sammoncrux*, the spell to gather them in one place and finally *Driglayor*, the spell to destroy them."

"Excellent work." Hermitus looked at Andreux with appreciation. "Let us get started."

As Hermitus chanted Indictora, Andreux saw red flickering lights on the wall swarming towards the tutelage. The tutelage looked like an island, surrounded by red water. With each spell, Andreux felt seismic turbulence and gushing winds. Then he witnessed several flashes of light that emanated from his master's wand, jetted through the roof and shot straight into the forest. He could see several sparks in the map

---

10　The words of this chant mean "Let me see on this wall what I desire to see."

of Aranya. There were loud screams, hissing sounds and moans. The red sparks disappeared and finally there was silence.

When the fight was over, Hermitus appeared fragile and beaten. But his face radiated with happiness. Andreux was jubilant that the creatures had been dealt with. He left the chamber and stepped out to meet his friends. Senfred and Pompompulous eagerly lapped up his narration of what had happened behind the master's closed doors.

Andreux described the fight in detail. They stood there for a long time and discussed the events that had taken place in the past lune. It was soon dusk. They quickly had supper and walked back to the master's chamber. They had many questions for him. But as they approached the chamber, the door opened and the stranger stepped out.

Andreux was surprised to see this. He and Senfred followed the stranger, who was walking rapidly to avoid being caught. As Andreux picked up his pace, a noise from behind caught his ears. When he turned to see what had caused the noise, he saw something else completely unexpected. The door to the master's chamber had opened again and his mother had stepped out.

Strangers come together when their fates destine.
Some become good friends, their destinies twine.
Some friendships are rare, true, deep and sublime,
those that withstand the tests of nature and time.

Many disciples made fun of Pompompulous's big, burly appearance, but he did not care about the rude comments or sneers of his fellow disciples. Nothing dampened his spirit. He had come there to study, and study he did. He was never interested in showing off his intelligence, so he remained known among fellow disciples only for his size. Only a few close friends, such as Andreux and Senfred, knew how resourceful he really was.

Once when Andreux and Senfred were both ill, Pompompulous volunteered to write study notes and complete assignments for them. However, Pompompulous soon realized that the assignment was very time-consuming. The next day when all the disciples handed in their notes, Hermitus noticed that Pompompulous did not submit his. When Hermitus asked him, Pompompulous explained that he did not have time to do his own assignment as he was busy trying to keep his word to his friends.

When he heard this, Hermitus brought this to every one's attention. "Here is a true example of what friendship means. Pompompulous has set aside his own needs to meet the needs of his friends. When you give your word to your friend, try to keep it, no matter what may come in your way."

Pompompulous was slightly embarrassed to hear his master praise him. No one had praised him in public before. That was partly because Pompompulous was never first at anything. He was also never the second or third. He was always somewhere towards the end. It had all started about two hogashes ago, when he had been born the sixth child to his parents. They had had one more a yedib later.

He was a late bloomer, always taking his time to appreciate life's basic principles. About a hogash after he was born, his younger brother surpassed him in physical and mental capabilities. That did not dampen the spirit of Pompompulous. In fact, he still remained carefree. That was his greatest gift, and his close friends admired him for it.

He was married when he was only one and three-quarters hogashes old. His wife, Rollmist, was the fifth among seven daughters, which made him the fifth son-in-law. In those days, sons-in-law were treated with respect. However, that was not the case with Pompompulous. Because he married into such a large family, by the time his in-laws took care of the needs of the first four sons-in-law, their time, energy and money were all spent. Pompompulous never minded the fact that his in-laws did not treat him with prompt attention and respect. On the contrary, he would joke about how worse off the sixth and seventh sons-in-law would be. Pompompulous always looked at the bright side.

He adored his wife. It was Rollmist who made him realize his untapped potential. He had a good memory, an excellent one, for that matter. He remembered everything, even the most vague and unimportant things. On their wedding night, when she had walked into his bedroom fully decked in jewels, his first comment had been, "My dear! How splendid you look! The colour of your jewels remind me of our neighbour's wife!"

Rollmist had not appeared to be amused with his statement.

"Are you having an affair with our neighbour's wife?" she'd asked.

Pompompulous was shocked. "How could you accuse me of such a thing?" he'd replied indignantly.

"Then why would you say such a thing?"

"I don't know. Somehow the colour of your jewels reminded me of her," he replied.

"How old is your neighbour's wife?"

"Not 'is' my dear, 'was.' She has been dead for many yedibs now," Pompompulous had replied, realizing that it was just a matter of unfounded jealousy. Rollmist had become quiet after that, and had not asked any other questions. The neighbour's wife had not come up as a topic for discussion until a lune later.

One day, after Pompompulous came home, tired of looking for a job, Rollmist had approached him from behind and hugged him, resting her head on his back. "I have some news for you," she'd said. "I've done some digging around to figure out why my jewels reminded you of your neighbour's wife."

Pompompulous turned to face her. "I thought we resolved the issue that night."

"Please hear me out. We only stopped talking about it; we never resolved anything. As I said, I made some discrete enquiries and found out that your neighbour sold all his wife's jewels to a merchant after her death. That merchant, in turn, sold them to my father, who gave them to me on our wedding day. You must have seen the old lady wearing the jewels before she died and remembered it subconsciously."

"So?" Pompompulous had replied nonchalantly.

"It shows you have an amazing memory, and you need to utilize it to make a name for yourself."

"Maybe I do!" exclaimed Pompompulous. No one, not even Pompompulous himself, had ever acknowledged his capabilities until that moment.

With Rollmist's encouragement, Pompompulous realized the potential of his memory. He remembered the names of all the kings that ever ruled the Vauntic kingdom. He remembered exactly when King Reganor was killed and when his son was born (including the positioning of the sun, moon and stars), even though he had been barely a half-hogash old himself. At that time, his father, a staunch supporter of the deceased king, had protested openly against Army Chief Nefarius when he had declared himself the king. As a result, Nefarius had imprisoned his father for a few yedibs.

Pompompulous also remembered how many times in his lifetime each customer had come to his father's shop and the various goods that his father sold to him. He would notice if anyone he had met changed their way of walking or talking.

While most children his own age went to a tutelage, Pompompulous had stayed behind. Pompompulous had toiled hard to support his family. When his father had been thrown into prison, the king had usurped their wealth. His mother taught him the basic principles of life, and that was all; she could afford nothing further.

But upon discovering his gift for recollection, Rollmist had encouraged him to pursue his education. "My father may not be wealthy, but he can easily take care of me while you study."

He had not agreed with her at first. "It is my duty as your husband to take care of your needs. I cannot let you become a burden to your parents." But he soon came to realize that once Rollmist made up her mind about something, it was very difficult to convince her otherwise. He had not spoken to her for several days, but Rollmist had been equally adamant. In the end, her will prevailed when Pompompulous realized that she had his interest at heart. That is how he had come to Hermitus's tutelage two yedibs ago.

Arianne had just stepped out of Hermitus's chamber, right after the stranger had left. Andreux and Senfred stood beside Pompompulous, who was intrigued as well; but he knew something that neither Andreux nor Senfred knew.

He could tell that Andreux was surprised to see his mother, and from the look on her face, she was surprised as well. Her face paled behind the veil, and for a flickering moment, Pompompulous could sense that she had not wanted to be caught off guard. Obviously, she had not wanted Andreux to see her.

After a few moments of awkward silence, he watched Andreux approach his mother and ask, "Mother, who was the person who just left?"

Arianne hesitated for a second. She then looked him squarely in the eye and said, "I will tell you everything very soon. Trust me." With that, she walked away to her chamber in the kitchen-cottage. Andreux's eyes followed her as she left. His silence betrayed his thoughts to Pompompulous. Pompompulous coughed a little to get his attention. It would have been hard to miss his cough in the otherwise-eerie silence that engulfed them, and Andreux and Senfred looked at him. Pompompulous cleared his throat.

"Surely you are bothered by this nocturnal visit. I'm not sure if this will help you, but I know something that you may want to know."

"What is it, Pompompulous?" Andreux held his mouth in a thin line.

"The stranger has been visiting the master every night for the past lune now," said Pompompulous. "And do you know what that means?"

"Andreux turned a hogash and a half a lune ago!" exclaimed Senfred.

Pompompulous looked approvingly at him.

"But what has that got to do with the stranger's visits?" asked Andreux.

"I'm not sure *how*, or for that matter even *if*, they are related. All I am saying is that it isn't a coincidence that the stranger first showed up here on the night of your birthday," said Pompompulous. After that, nothing else was said, but long into the night, each of the three friends lay awake with his thoughts.

The next day, as soon as Pompompulous woke up, he went straight to his friends. Noticing that Andreux had already gone, he woke up Senfred. Senfred was not amused.

"The day has not yet started. It better be good, Pompompulous," he cautioned his friend.

"It is. Trust me."

Then there was silence.

"Well?" Senfred looked enquiringly at Pompompulous.

"About what we were discussing last night …" Pompompulous paused. He did not know how to put it. Maybe he should talk about it with Andreux rather than Senfred, he thought; it had more to do with Andreux, after all. It seemed fair.

"And?" Senfred was apparently losing his patience.

"Nothing I guess," said Pompompulous as he walked away, lost in his thoughts. He knew that the stranger would be visiting the master again that evening. Last night, when he was returning to the master's chamber from the kitchen, he had heard voices coming from inside. The first speaker's voice had not sounded familiar.

"I'll see you tomorrow at the same time, Revered Master."

"I'll wait for you." Pompompulous had recognized his master's voice.

"It will be an important day for all of us." Then the door opened and the stranger stepped out of the chamber.

As he lay awake that night, Pompompulous figured that Andreux's past would be revealed the next night. He wasn't sure if he was right this time, but he wanted to share his hunch with Andreux, so he went looking for him.

First he went to the wooden bridge. That was Andreux's favourite spot. Andreux often stood in the middle of the bridge, which swayed back and forth very lightly. The view was breathtaking as the river shone brightly when the sunlight or moonlight hit it. The sun was just about to rise and the moon was still visible in the now-orange skies. The forest on the banks reflected in the river waters. But Pompompulous did not find Andreux there.

Then he looked for him at the animal farm. Andreux loved to spend time taking care of the master's animals, especially his deer. Andreux was not there, either. Intuitively, Pompompulous went to the abandoned cave. Though Hermitus had not lifted the ban, the friends knew that it was now safe to step outside the tutelage. Andreux was standing next to the cave entrance, lost in thought. Pompompulous walked towards him and felt something prick him in the arm—a rather unusually large thorn. He pulled it out, tossed it away and continued his search.

Pompompulous desperately wanted to tell his friend what he had heard last night. But as he approached Andreux, a strange feeling took over Pompompulous. His friendly nature was suppressed; he became withdrawn and did not feel like talking to Andreux anymore. He suddenly realized he wanted to find out for himself if the stranger would indeed reveal Andreux's secret past tonight. He walked back to the tutelage, rather puzzled as to why he even bothered to find Andreux in the first place. Tonight's meeting was his secret, and he would be the first to know whatever it was.

Later that night, Pompompulous went to his master's dwelling. He knew that Hermitus would not be in his chamber at that time. He went in quickly and closed the door. He looked for a safe hiding spot, but there were hardly any worldly possessions in the chamber.

There was a small writing table, but it was so close to the ground one had to sit on the floor to write on it. Then there was the shelf next to a wall, which stored Hermitus's garments. Again, it was too small for Pompompulous—or anyone for that matter. The only thing that could hide his overgrown body was the bed. The bed squeaked as he slipped under it. It was quite uncomfortable, but Pompompulous did not worry, as he knew it would not be very long before the stranger would pay his next visit.

No sooner had Pompompulous hid under the bed than Hermitus entered the chamber and locked the door. Pompompulous did not expect this. How was the stranger expected to meet with Hermitus if the door was locked? At the same time, he felt as if an invisible layer was being lifted off his mind. He started to question why he was hiding like a thief in his master's chamber. After a few moments of self-interrogation, Pompompulous decided to come clean with his master. Just then, a noise from behind took him by surprise. He turned around as noiselessly as possible to find the source.

The wall between the bedroom and the study was opening up as if it were a door. When it opened wide enough, the stranger stepped out of it. The wall then closed back to its original position. Pompompulous was so taken aback that he let out a slight gasp. Luckily, his gasp went unnoticed.

As the stranger went to greet Hermitus, Pompompulous realized that though he had always seen the stranger leaving the chamber, never had he seen him enter from the outside. Now he knew why! Andreux and Senfred had lost track of him in the forest because of a secret passage that the stranger must have been using. And that led to Hermitus's chamber!

The stranger extended his hand to Hermitus, who greeted him with a brief but warm hug. Then they both sat down on two stools facing each other. Hermitus's back faced the bed under which Pompompulous lay. The stranger sat in front of him, his face partly visible. He had thick moustache and beard, just as Andreux had described. However,

Pompompulous had seen the stranger's face without the beard as a child in Vauns. He recognized the stranger instantly.

He was the ex-minister of Vauns, now in exile and wanted by the current king, Nefarius. Pompompulous had seen his face on several painted-cloth announcements displayed in the busy marketplace in his hometown. Nefarius had announced a reward for anyone who captured the ex-minister, dead or alive. Pompompulous knew that the king would rather have him dead than alive. His father had once made him take an oath to protect this man, as he was noble and respected by men in the kingdom. But what was the ex-minister doing here? Was his master sheltering a fugitive? Before Pompompulous could speculate any more, the men began talking.

"Do you have any new developments today, Minister Veritus?"

"I do and I don't, Sage Hermitus," replied Veritus. "I have been able to assemble part of the army that fought directly under King Reganor and swore allegiance to him and his kin. As you know, it has taken several days to get the message out. I had to use discretion."

"This is wonderful news. Why are you sceptical, then?" enquired Hermitus.

"I was also hoping to get the message to the soldiers in exile who have resolved to banditry in the past few yedibs. I am not exaggerating when I say that my success will likely depend on the support of this contingent of the army."

"And I am not exaggerating when I say that what you have managed to do in the past few days is almost impossible. So keep up the good work. The last piece of the puzzle will also fall into place," said Hermitus encouragingly.

"I most certainly hope so. I have been waiting for this day for such a long time. If you had not helped us, I would have been captured a long time ago. And the royal family—"

At that very moment, Pompompulous heard a sharp hissing near him. He turned to see a black spotted rattlesnake under the bed next to him, looking into his eyes. When he saw the snake, he panicked, let out a loud cry and jumped out from under the bed.

Veritus stopped talking, pulled out his sword and held it to Pompompulous's neck. Pompompulous thought he was about to lose his head, when Hermitus stopped him. "He is my disciple, Minister Veritus. A harmless one."

Veritus's sword cut the snake into two pieces. He then studied Pompompulous. "I know him by his father. I am glad that I have not harmed the son of Prosperus."

Pompompulous fell at his master's feet. He was shaking with fear, first for almost being bit by the snake and next for being caught red-handed. He asked for his master's forgiveness and bowed in reverence to the ex-minister.

"Now, Pompompulous. What were you doing under my bed at this time of the night-sun?" asked Hermitus.

Pompompulous was so nervous he babbled out everything. "I'm sorry, Master. I had seen the ex-minister leave your chamber for the past few nights. I overheard, by accident, the last few words of your conversation. Andreux mentioned that his mother would reveal his past soon. So when I found Aunt Arianne leaving the chamber last night, I put two and two together. This morning I went to talk to Andreux, but for some reason, I left without telling him anything. I'm not sure why curiosity got the better of me, but I managed to sneak into your chamber and hide under the bed to find out the secret for myself. That is all, Master." After he was finished, he lowered his head in shame. "I am ready to accept any punishment you may deem my misbehaviour warrants. But I can assure, Master, that I will never divulge the secret of the Honourable Minister. I have sworn on my father's life."

"I wouldn't go that far, Pompompulous. I am not sure what came over you. I would like you to fetch Andreux and Senfred to my chamber immediately."

"Master, may I ask—"

"You will know everything in a few moments, Pompompulous. Now please bring them to my chamber."

"But Master, is it advisable to involve an outsider?" Veritus asked as Pompompulous moved to leave.

"He is already involved. And I trust him. Moreover, she trusts him like her own son. Maybe he is destined to play a part in the story that will soon unfold," replied Hermitus.

As Pompompulous stepped out of his master's chamber, he saw Arianne walking towards the master's chamber. She no longer had her face covered under a veil. It shone like a thousand moons and he recognized her in an instant. He bowed to her.

"At your service, Your Royal Highness Queen Minerva!" he said, bent on one knee. The question that he wanted to ask Hermitus in the chamber was answered. His heart was elated.

She placed her hand on his shoulder. "You are my son's friend and will always be, Pompompulous. Your master must be waiting for you to fetch Andreux and Senfred. Don't keep him waiting," she said, and she stepped into the chamber.

How did she know? Pompompulous was intrigued. Things were happening too fast. Now he knew why she always had her face covered with a veil. His blood boiled to think of all the plights and troubles that she had gone through all these yedibs. Nefarius must pay the price for all of that.

As he ran to fetch his friends, he couldn't decide whether to tell them about ex-minister Veritus. He was very eager to tell them everything that he knew; at the same time he thought it would be appropriate if he left that to the elders. *This must surely be the moment that the queen has been waiting for all these yedibs,* he thought. He chose to remain tight-lipped until they reached the chamber. There was one small piece of the puzzle that did not seem to fit, but he was so overwhelmed by the recent revelations that he ignored it. He would have his answers very soon.

Chapter Five
Prince in Exile

What you perceive just may not be true.
What you thought you knew could be a lie through and through.
The secrets that you don't know may baffle you.
Your existence could change in a monnet or two.

Oblivious to what had happened in the master's chamber, Andreux was assisting Senfred with the kitchen chores, by arranging the washed dishes in the shelves. Out of the blue, he asked, "What was the matter with Pompompulous earlier today?" All he got back in response was a nonchalant "Tell me about it."

"He was not his usual self. First he walked towards me, full of excitement. The next moment, he just walked away. I wonder what is the matter with him?"

Senfred did not respond.

Andreux noticed his disinterest and decided to change the topic. "It seems that I finally have some free time," he told Senfred as they walked out of the kitchen.

"The last few days *have* been busy, with the food theft and the half-world creature scare," replied Senfred.

"And not to mention helping Master fight the half-world creatures," said Andreux.

"At least you got to help. I wasn't involved at all. I couldn't even talk to you to find out what was happening because you were so busy," said Senfred.

"Oh, I meant to tell you, I think something was wrong with Glimp this morning."

"What happened?" asked Senfred.

"First, he asked me to meet him at the abandoned cave. When I get there, there was no sign of him. In fact, that's where I found Pompompulous acting strangely."

"Something's going on. And you can't trust Glimp. He has always been on Nevius's side," Senfred remarked just as Pompompulous approached.

"Here you are, both of you. The master wants to meet with you in his chamber—right now." His last two words tweaked Andreux's curiosity

"What's so urgent?" asked Senfred.

"How am I supposed to know? As if he tells me everything! I'm just the messenger."

"What's up with you? You've been acting strange all day." Senfred looked at him, his brows knotted together in a frown.

"I know. I haven't been myself lately. And I need to apologize for that." As Pompompulous was talking, they passed Glimp, who was so engrossed in his conversation with himself that he did not notice who was approaching. Pompompulous put his index finger to his lips and gestured for his friends to be quiet. As usual, Glimp was talking about Nevius.

"I wish we could somehow stop getting mixed up with Nevius," complained Glimp.

"But at the same time, I don't want to lose my chances with him either," said Glimp again, in a voice quite unlike his own. It was as if he was having a conversation with himself!

"You better decide whose side you'll be on, because the judgement day is near," said Pompompulous, grabbing Glimp with his strong hands.

Glimp shrieked with fear. "Of course we're on your side, Pompompulous. Why would you think otherwise?" Pompompulous rolled his eyes at Glimp's assurance.

"Don't try to get clever with me. You're as much to be blamed for Nevius's schemes as he is. If you weren't busy covering up his crimes, he would've been expelled a long time ago. I bet that the food disappearing from the kitchen had something to do with him."

Glimp almost choked, so Andreux intervened and told Pompompulous to let him go.

"Thank you, Andreux, for saving my life. Now we're even," said Glimp.

"What do you mean by that?" asked Andreux.

"Well, just to prove that we're good people, let me tell you what happened this morning. Nevius is still wandering around the tutelage, and he wanted to kill you with the cobra poison. This morning, while you were at the cave, he threw a thorn dipped in its poison at you," Glimp tried to explain in his hoarse voice.

"You mean to say that he actually poisoned Andreux?" screamed Senfred.

"No. I didn't say that. I was just saying that he threw the thorn at Andreux—"

Andreux interrupted him. "Now stop right there. You were the one who took me there this morning. So you actually helped Nevius by almost getting me killed. Then why are we even?" He raised his fist.

"Have some mercy. Let us finish. Nevius failed. The thorn pricked Pompompulous, who happened to get in its way—"

"I'm sorry, I didn't know of your plans and sorry for ruining them. Had I known then—" Pompompulous paused for a moment. "So that was what pricked me. Now that makes sense. I was beginning to wonder." Then he paused again. His face turned red as the realization dawned upon him. "You mean to say I've been given the kiss of death?" He grabbed Glimp's by the neck and started shaking him violently.

"Let us finish. If it were poison, would you still be alive?" asked Glimp. Pompompulous's grip relaxed. Glimp coughed a little and continued. "It's true that the thorn pricked Pompompulous. But it didn't have the cobra venom as Nevius was hoping. I cleverly switched it with the dark-slider venom."

"You need to slow down and explain everything." urged Senfred.

Glimp elaborated thus: "The other day, I was walking towards the river when Nevius found me. I had helped him in the past, things that I am not proud of, and Nevius threatened to expose those misdeeds if I did not go along with him. He said he wanted to kill Andreux with the snake venom. If he could not study at the tutelage, neither could Andreux. He wanted my help. My job was to coat the thorn with Negi poison, fetch Andreux and bring him to the abandoned cave.

"As you know, Andreux, I talked you into coming to the cave, but as soon as we reached the cave, I got cold feet. You stayed, while I fled the scene. I cleverly switched Nevius's poison with my own, that of the dark-slider. I knew it wouldn't kill Andreux. So what Nevius assumed to be Negi's poison was in fact dark-slider's venom. As soon as Nevius threw the thorn, I ran away.

"Nevius threw the thorn at Andreux. Pompompulous took the hit instead. Seeing what he had done, Nevius quickly left the scene. He would've gladly thrown another thorn at Andreux, but he had no more. I had emptied Nevius's container and convinced him that the poison had dried up. But I'm glad that you're alive."

"The dark-slider poison changes behaviour! That's why I was acting strange!" exclaimed Pompompulous. He then looked at Glimp. "You almost got me into trouble with the master," he said. "But why did you save Andreux's life?"

"Whatever the reason, we're thankful to you. We will remain indebted to you for what you've done today," said Andreux. He could tell Glimp was embarrassed for being thanked.

"Well, it was nothing, actually. I was a friend of Nevius, but I was not your enemy. And I would never wish for anyone to die," he said modestly. The three friends thanked him again and walked towards the chamber.

Before Pompompulous opened the door, Senfred asked, "So, 'Pulous, what is this about?"

"Well, why don't you find out for yourself?" Pompompulous replied with a smile, ushering his friends inside.

As he entered the chamber Andreux's eyes locked with the stranger's. It was the same face he had seen in darkness. *Why did the man run away from me that night, yet he stands boldly in front of me now?* he wondered. He was shocked to see his mother in the chamber without the veil covering her face. He bowed to the man, his mother and Hermitus. Hermitus asked everyone to sit, and he secured the lock on the door to prevent unwanted intrusions. "This must be very important," whispered Senfred.

"Andreux and Senfred, may I introduce you to Veritus, the ex-minister of Vauns?" Andreux and Senfred looked at each other in disbelief. Then Andreux looked over at Pompompulous, who was beaming.

Pompompulous leaned over and said, "Wait for the best part. It's not over yet."

Andreux raised his eyebrows. *What are they up to?*

Hermitus continued. "And Veritus, this is Andreux, son of King Reganor and Queen Minerva, your prince in exile."

Andreux stood up, speechless. He wanted to ask so many things at once.

Veritus looked at him from head to toe. "Please accept my respects, O Prince." he said as he bowed slightly.

"Please call me Andreux. You're older than me."

The minister smiled slightly. "Just like your father. I cannot tell you how glad I am to see you tonight. I have waited all these yedibs and thought that this moment would never come. But I did not give up hope."

Andreux turned his gaze towards his mother and realized she was fighting hard to control her tears. He walked up to her and held her, and she burst out crying. He was still trying to comprehend what he had just been told. He could not bear to see his mother in anguish.

"Finally, the moment that you and I have been waiting for so long has arrived, my son. I only wish your father were here with us. He would've been so proud of you."

"If my father was the King of Vauns, why didn't you tell me? Why did we have to live in exile?"

"The minister will answer all your questions in a moment, Andreux," intervened Hermitus, "but the introductions are not yet over." He looked at Senfred. "And Veritus, this is Senfred, your son."

Neither Andreux nor Senfred was prepared for this. Andreux expected to wake up any minute. He watched as Veritus hugged his son. Senfred's tears flowed and whatever questions or hesitation Andreux had had earlier melted away. He was sure that Senfred had many questions, just like him, but words failed them both. Things were happening too quickly, and he wanted to savour every moment.

"Now that the introductions are complete, let us take this moment to reflect on the past," said Hermitus. "I imagine that Andreux and Senfred have many questions. In their best interests, we have kept them in the dark all these yedibs. But now it is time to reveal their past to them. Minister Veritus, since you have been the actual witness to most of the events, I request that you narrate the events that have led to their exile."

Veritus cleared his throat, looked at every one in the chamber and began.

"It all started about a yedib before Prince Andreux was born. I had received information from reliable sources that Army Chief Nefarius was resorting to bribing the soldiers in his army to gain their support and ultimately dethrone the king. I created a false rumour that there were uprisings in the border communities and that lives were being lost due to attacks from neighbouring kingdoms. I let the rumours float for some time and then had the king send Nefarius to resolve the problem with a small contingent of the army. While he was gone, I wasted little time in regaining the faith and allegiance of most of the army. That was when my wife gave birth to Senfred; she died soon thereafter."

Veritus stopped and looked at Senfred. Andreux noticed immense pain in both pairs of eyes.

"Your mother was very dear to me, Senfred. She gave you your name. She would have been proud of you, my son. When she died, a part of me died. But you gave me a renewed purpose to live." He looked at everyone gathered in the chamber and continued.

"The king and queen were very supportive during that phase of my life. The queen took care of Senfred as if he were her own child. That gave me time to set right the wrongdoings of Nefarius. With the little time I had left, I played with Senfred and watched him grow. After a few meths, the queen became pregnant. There were celebrations everywhere. I had to take special precautions to make sure Nefarius did not get this message. That would have caused unnecessary tensions at that time. But, as I realized later, there were still some soldiers in the army who were on his side and were keeping him informed of everything that was going on in his absence.

"On the day that Prince Andreux was born, the king and queen were happy beyond words. The entire city was festive, with homes and streets decked in colourful flowers and lamps. People flocked into the streets and sang and danced all day. The king was very tired at the end of the day and retired to bed early. I was still keeping a close eye on the proceedings when a soldier came running down the stairs of the patrol tower, gasping for breath. He informed me that Nefarius was marching back into the city with his army. I immediately sensed trouble and ran to the palace to tighten security. I alerted the chief of guards. The queen's chamber was the closest to where I was, and so I went to warn her.

"She was exhausted from childbirth, holding the baby in her arms, while the common folk and royal dignitaries alike visited her with greetings, blessings and gifts. She could barely keep awake when I went into her chamber, but when I cautioned her, she was immediately prepared for the worst. She got out of her bed, holding the prince in one arm and Senfred in the other. I asked her to lock all doors to her chamber from the inside and not to open them until she heard from me. If I succeeded in averting a coup, I would personally come and ask her to open the door. If by any chance I failed in my mission, I will ring the bell three times at the patrol tower. I told her to escape through the secret tunnel from her chamber that would lead to the forest near this tutelage." Veritus paused to look at Senfred.

"Though I had no sisters, she was more than one to me. I did not know if I would see you again so I took a long look at you all. Then I went to the king's chamber. As I approached his chamber, I saw someone running towards me. Not knowing who it was from that distance, I pulled out my sword, prepared to fight. But it turned out to be Religer, the royal prophet. He told me he had some doubts about the prince's future and had left back home after all the other prophets prophesied a glorious future for the prince and the kingdom under his rule. He had checked his parchments and realized that the star positions at the prince's birth time indicated a very turbulent childhood. He had come to warn the king.

"I assured the prophet that I would pass on his message to the king and asked him to return home right away as the turbulence he was predicting had already started. Then I ran to the king's chamber. But the crime had already been committed. The guards who were patrolling the chamber lay dead on the floor. With a sinking feeling, I opened the door to the king's bedroom. The bed was in a disarray, bearing witness to the struggle that must have occurred there. There was blood everywhere. The king had been murdered. But I could not find his body. I ran immediately to the patrol tower and rang the bell three times, hoping the queen would get my message before it was too late.

"Hiding from my enemy, I ran from chamber to chamber looking for any trace of the king. I could not find him. In one chamber, I heard the followers of Nefarius talking. I hid behind a pillar and listened. One of the men was saying how he had killed the king and thrown his body down the mountain. The other said that they were still searching for me, the queen and Andreux. I was pained to hear of the king's demise, but I was relieved to hear that the queen was safe. As they continued to talk, my blood boiled and I jumped at them with a sword in my hand. I was so overcome with emotions that I did not care how many soldiers were in the room. I killed them all, one after the other. Soon the room filled up with their dead bodies. Realizing that I was running against time, I decided to run from the city as well. I was sure Nefarius would put out a heavy reward for my head."

Andreux nodded. For the first time everything was beginning to make sense.

"I ran straight to the tutelage. The queen was already there with her attendant, the ever-faithful Sitafore, who carried the prince and Senfred. The queen fainted when I told her the king had met an untimely death. I worried if she would survive the ordeal, but she lived with determination and fortitude. She had been actively involved with the king in ruling the kingdom and she did not want to see all their efforts wash away in vain. She wanted to see Prince Andreux crowned as king one day.

"Master Hermitus was kind enough to let her stay at the tutelage with the two infants. Sitafore stayed back here under the assumed name of Mandrill. I could not stay here as I had a great deal of work to accomplish if the queen's plans were to be realized. I had to maintain and foster hope among the king's followers and mobilize forces to fight Nefarius. I visited Hermitus periodically to keep him posted of recent developments and also to see you both grow up. I returned to the city every now and then during the past hogash and a half, and the reward on our heads has continued to increase. The reward to find the royal family and myself now stands at a hefty sum of 99,716 gold medallions.

"The hope of seeing the prince crowned one day kept me going all these yedibs. The queen instilled faith in me whenever I returned to the tutelage full of despair and anguish. I have been honoured to have known her and the king. I have sworn to spend the rest of my life in their service."

He bowed to the queen again. There was silence for a few awkward moments.

"Why did you have to live in the cave for the past few days?" Andreux asked.

"An excellent question. Somehow Nefarius came to know about the secret meetings that I was conducting in the city. He put parchments at all important trade centres and village halls, denouncing me as a traitor. Anyone who tried to help me would be punished with death. The security in the city was tightened; therefore, I had to lie low for a few days. I also wanted to take this opportunity to reveal the truth to you. However, that was delayed by the news of half-world creatures. As the cave was connected to this chamber, it worked out well."

Queen Minerva took a step forward. "We had to wait until you were a hogash and a half old, my son. That would mark the completion of your studies. Also, that was the age when you could be crowned the king."

"Nefarius had offered a lot of money to know your whereabouts, so we all had to keep the past a secret to keep you safe. Nebulus, father of Nevius, is still hiring spies to look for the royal family in exile," Veritus informed Andreux.

Andreux's fist tightened when he heard this. "You've suffered a lot on our account. I'm humbled by your unwavering loyalty, as well as deeply disturbed by the pain that our families and countless others have endured all these yedibs. If only I could—" Andreux was choked with emotions.

Hermitus patted him gently on his shoulders. "Andreux, compose yourself, my child. The day to right the wrong is very close. We are all very proud of how you have turned out. Your education is now complete. The last thing that you needed to learn was Atmaitika. I wish you the best in your life and endeavours," he said.

He then looked at Senfred and Pompompulous. "You both have always exceeded my expectations and will make your loved ones proud. I have taught you everything that you could possibly need in future. Your education is also complete."

Andreux and his friends bowed their heads to their master and stood with folded hands as a sign of respect. "I thank you, Minister, for your sacrifices," said Andreux.

"Please do not keep thanking me," replied Veritus.

"Let him, Veritus. He is trying to come to grips with reality. He is beginning to acknowledge what happened to us," said Minerva.

Senfred looked solemn. "Did you miss me father?" he asked.

"Yes my child. Your image was the one hope that kept me going all these yedibs," Veritus replied and, addressing Minerva, he said, "I cannot thank you enough for looking after my son as your own."

"It has been my pleasure, Veritus," replied Minerva as she affectionately put her hand on Senfred's head.

"How was my childhood before all this happened? What did my mother look like? How did you live all these yedibs?" Questions poured out of Senfred, and Veritus answered them patiently, as they had a lot to catch up.

"Father, I remember Mandrill telling us about a stranger chasing Nevius. Was that you, by any chance?" Senfred asked.

"It was me. I mistook him to be a spy from Nefarius's army loitering around the tutelage," replied Veritus.

Andreux also had many questions for his mother. "What did father look like, mother?" he asked her.

Minerva showed him a portrait of Reganor that she had hidden in the master's chamber all these yedibs.

Andreux bowed to the portrait. Then he held it in his arms and cried. His wish to know who his father was had come true, but he was not destined to meet his father in person.

Minerva consoled him. "Your father was kind-hearted, intelligent, brave and wise, Andreux! His subjects loved him as much as he loved them. I am not sure why he met with such a cruel fate; he certainly did not deserve it. Ah! The mere memory of his death is hard to mention." She wept softly.

Andreux held her in an embrace. He wished he knew his father more. He was also angry that his father had been murdered in cold blood. "I will reclaim his kingdom and avenge his death," he vowed.

Minerva spoke firmly. "You will do nothing in haste that we would all regret later. That was another reason why you were not informed of our past all these yedibs. The enemy is waiting for a sign to reveal our existence and we are not ready to give away any indication to him, not yet."

"I suggest that you keep this meeting a secret," Hermitus said. "I will now request that everyone retire for the night and reconvene tomorrow morning. We have a lot of ground to cover tomorrow. We will be discussing our immediate course of action in much greater detail."

Chapter Six
Best-Laid Plans

Some lives are wasted in pomp and luxury.
Wretched are some lives, drenched in misery.
Some live in exile, whilst some lives are free.
Some lead lives of mission, some are carefree.

By the time, Andreux, Senfred and Pompompulous got to the disciples' chamber, it was dark and everyone else had fallen asleep.

"I know a lot about the past from my father. He always openly discussed various matters with us at supper time. How we looked forward to having supper with him! He is a true patriot and has always stood for what he believed," whispered Pompompulous.

"Tell us more about him, 'pulous," requested Andreux.

"When I was young, about a half-hogash, my father, Prosperus, was the richest merchant in the city. He sent ships to far away kingdoms and filled them up with merchandise that was not available in Vauns. While on one such voyage, he heard that the king was murdered and Nefarius was proclaiming himself to be the king.

"He was upset when he heard this news. He returned to Vauns immediately, without completing his business transactions. On his way back, he sent a message that asked my uncle to make arrangements for my father to meet with his friends to discuss their future plans. Unfortunately, my uncle had already defected to Nefarius's camp and he passed on this information to Nefarius.

"Imagine the surprise of my father, when his vessel reached the shores of the Vauntic Sea! He certainly did not expect the king's soldiers waiting to capture him. When they dragged him to the court, people gathered in the street to catch a glimpse of the fate that befell Vauns's most successful merchant. My mother heard the commotion and enquired what the matter was. She had been expecting my father to return home that day. No one knew what my evil uncle had done!

When she realized what had become of my father, she ran to the streets to meet him. The soldiers pushed her away. My father was sentenced to three yedibs in prison, without even getting a chance to prove his innocence. Though he was loyal to Reganor, he never betrayed Nefarius. However he was accused of evading tolls and duties over the past hogash, resulting in lost revenues to the king's treasury.

"The next three yedibs were hell for us. Nefarius seized my father's vessels and merchandise. We had to sell our house to pay off the suppliers. I could not afford to study because I had to work along with my brothers to prevent the family from starving.

"Every night I would ask my mother why father was imprisoned and what had happened to the royal family. She told me the same story every night. It was more or less what Minister Veritus narrated earlier, but there were a few other facts that she would mention.

"First, Nefarius had some informers inside and outside the army. My uncle was one of them. When the queen became pregnant, a messenger was sent to Nefarius to alert him. Somehow the messenger never reached Nefarius. By the time his disappearance became known, it was only a few meths before the queen would deliver the baby. Another messenger was sent in a great panic, this time a woman. She must have managed to deliver the message, because Nefarius returned to the city the night before you, Andreux, were born.

"He met with his supporters at my uncle's house that night. They planned to get rid of the entire royal family and whoever came in the way of their plans. They also planned to get rid of Minister Veritus. They would carry out their plans while the kingdom was busy celebrating the birth of the newborn.

"Meanwhile, one of my father's friends, who was also loyal to King Reganor, came to know about this secret meeting and he witnessed the entire proceedings without their knowledge. However, just as they were about to leave, they discovered his presence and killed him then and there. They also warned my uncle of dire consequences if he told anyone else. I suspect they did not believe him completely because of my father's known loyalty to King Reganor.

"We were unaware of all this. It was much later, after my father was thrown in prison, that my uncle came to our house, under the influence of wine and bragged about how he got my father in prison. My brothers beat him to a pulp, but that did not change my father's situation. It was too late to do anything by then.

"My father spent three yedibs in prison, thanks to my uncle's treachery. He did not spend his time in vain. He quickly realized that there were a lot of prisoners like him, who loathed Nefarius and sympathized with what had happened to the royal family. He quickly started a movement within the dark walls of the dungeon that had become their home. They called themselves the Vauntic Army and made elaborate plans to get rid of Nefarius once they were all released. But the only problem was that no one seemed to know where the royal family was.

"When my father finally walked out of the dark dungeons to smell the fresh air, he was more determined than ever to fight for the cause of King Reganor. He returned to us for a brief time to make sure that we were taking care of ourselves in his absence. I still treasure that time. He would spend all night talking to us about his plans. He instilled a sense of pride and purpose in our lives. He told us that we were able to live lives of luxury when King Reganor lived. The royal family was now living somewhere in exile while we still managed to live in the city even if we'd had to give up most of our comforts. He made us swear allegiance to the royal family in exile. He was outraged when he knew that my uncle, his brother, had helped Nefarius all along. The night before he went into hiding with his friends and supporters, we stayed up all night and talked and talked. We were not sure when or if we would see him again."

Andreux bowed his head. So many people had suffered so that he could live. He would live to repay them for what they had done.

"The day after his departure, there were random attacks on the supporters of Nefarius. My uncle narrowly escaped an attack on his life. Others were not so lucky. Nefarius fortified the city with more soldiers. My father retreated to the jungles that surrounded the fort and stayed there with his friends and supporters. Every now and then, we would get messages of his safety and where he was in his planning. Slowly they stopped coming, because if the king's henchmen intercepted them, it would cost them their lives.

"There were several rumours about the whereabouts of the royal family, but no one actually saw them. There were huge rewards announced by Nefarius for any information that led to their capture. But that did not help either.

"In the yedibs that passed, Nefarius plundered the kingdom. His henchmen openly looted honest subjects and amassed their wealth. Ex-Minister Veritus was also working hard to cause an uprising, but there were two big obstacles. First, the royal family was in exile. The people needed to know that they were still alive in order to support any such uprising. This was difficult, my father often noted in his messages, as any slight hint of their whereabouts may lead to their capture and death. Also the prince, if he was alive, had to be at least one and one-half hogashes old in order to claim the throne. Secondly, Nefarius built his army by distributing his loot among his soldiers. They were united in their efforts to protect him. The supporters of King Reganor were divided and did not have enough financial resources to fight Nefarius, whose army had access to the royal treasury. With each passing yedib, the open support for the royal family seemed to dwindle.

"Thus it's been more than a hogash since I've seen my father. We do get messages from him every once in a while to confirm he's still alive. My uncle lives in a mansion, while the rest of my family barely manages to make ends meet." Pompompulous wiped the tears off his face.

Andreux was amazed to know that they had so many supporters who were fighting for them. His admiration for Pompompulous grew when he realized how much his family suffered over the yedibs. "I wish I had known from the start. I shouldn't have been kept in the dark," he said sadly.

"I know. I should've been with my father all this time," said Senfred. "But they have all sacrificed their lives for a bigger cause. Now that we know our past, it's time to bring justice to our families and to the kingdom."

Andreux shrugged. "It must have pained my mother each time she looked at us. I'm not complaining about my life here. I'll always be grateful for everything I've learnt here. But I only wish I knew my destiny a little earlier."

"It's never too late. Now that we know who we are, and now that you are one and one-half hogashes, I think it's time to finish the task our parents set in motion so many yedibs ago," said Senfred.

"I'm thankful to Rollmist for sending me to study. Otherwise I would never have had a chance to meet such good friends, who will very soon be the next king and minister. I hope that Nefarius will soon be removed from the throne. Only that would reunite me with my father," said Pompompulous.

Andreux and Senfred both thanked him for the pain and suffering his family had been going through all these yedibs.

"This exile will end very soon. When we meet with the minister tomorrow, we will plan for the final attack on Nefarius," Andreux assured him.

Senfred added, "You'll always be with us, no matter where we end up."

The next morning, the three friends were eager to hear more. They could not wait to meet with Veritus, who had remained in the tutelage. They all sat down for breakfast; Senfred, for his first breakfast with his father.

"Where did you live all these yedibs, father?" he asked.

"In no one place for more than a few days, my son. It was truly the life of a nomad. Even though many well-wishers offered to keep me in their homes and guard my presence with absolute secrecy, I could not put them at risk of losing their lives in the dungeons, or losing their property to Nefarius. My life's mission has been to put together an army by the time the prince turns a hogash and a half. I could not risk losing my life or that of others, at least not until my mission was accomplished.

"The cruelties that were being inflicted upon the subjects in Vauns have only increased with time. Most of them are now living in abject poverty. Some have lost their lives' savings, while others have lost their lives."

Andreux was agitated when he heard this. His face reddened with rage and his breathing quickened. His hand went to his sword. "The people of Vauns have suffered enough. It's time for justice to prevail. Let us waste no more time. The time to avenge is upon us," he declared.

"I want revenge, not just for myself, but for everyone who suffered under the new king."

Minerva put her hand on his arm. "Andreux, I implore you to be calm. These sudden outbursts make me anxious. I plead with you to remain patient and listen to what the minister has to say."

Everyone's attention turned to Veritus.

The minister pulled out a hand-drawn map from his bag. The map was drawn using charcoal on a dried papyrus. It was crumpled and showed signs of wear. He spread it out on the wall and the map remained there without having to be nailed.

"The time to topple the king is very near," he said, looking at everyone in the room. Everyone was looking at the map, trying to absorb as much information as possible.

"Let me explain the map to you," Veritus started. He pointed to the map. "This is the tutelage, where we are right now. It is surrounded by the forest Aranya, for the most part. There are a few ways, outlined here, that would lead us from the tutelage to the kingdoms that surround it. As you can see, the forest has three kingdoms on three sides. Our kingdom, Vauns, is to its east, Appaun lies to its west and Attyme lies to its south. There are three paths from the forest that lead to Vauns. The army of Nefarius heavily guards one of them, as this path lies on the border with Attyme. The other is a secret passage that leads straight into the palace chambers. This one is risky as well, as Nefarius knows parts of it. The third one is the safest and the longest path. As you can see for yourselves, this path meanders through the dense forest of Aranya.

"The forest shelters not only wild animals but also magical creatures, demons and ogres. Though Hermitus cleansed the forest of half-world creatures, those ogres and demons that did not swear allegiance to the Lord of Darkness and Evil still roam freely in Aranya. There are a few spots marked with an *x* on the map along this path through the forest. These are the intermediary checkpoints that you need to look out for. The checkpoints will prevent you from getting lost. As you can see, there are several landmarks along the way that will help you stay on course. If you miss any of them, you have to retrace your steps to the previous checkpoint. There is, however, a dilapidated shelter that is now the abode of an ogress as well as a ruined relic that you must avoid at all costs. Near the ruined relic is a huge Capirona tree, which is the tallest in the forest. You need to climb it during daylight to find out your way to Vauns. You can break the journey for the night near the riverbed, which is by far the safest resting point known to me."

Veritus waited for Andreux to nod. When he did, Veritus continued. "I want you to visit the kingdom and get a feel for it yourself. The subjects are waiting to see that the prince is ready to claim the crown. I have managed to unite most of the soldiers in exile, except for one major faction. While you visit Vauns, I will make a final pitch to get this faction on our side." He then handed Andreux a bag of gold coins.

"You might need this. As I warned you before, Nefarius has announced a large reward for your capture. I still have to gather the support of the main contingent of Reganor's army living in exile, so I will be preoccupied with that for the next day or two. I will meet you at Religer's home on the third day from now. Use these gold coins with judgement."

"If the master and minister do not object, I would like to follow Andreux and Senfred to Vauns and make my father proud," Pompompulous said.

Hermitus nodded. "As I mentioned last night, your education here in the tutelage is now complete, Pompompulous. It is now entirely up to you to make proper use of it in life."

Pompompulous bowed to his teacher.

Veritus patted him on his back. "It is heartening to see patriotism in the new generation, Pompompulous. Your father's loyalty and support have been invaluable for us all these yedibs. I am sure your knowledge of the outlay of the city of Vauns will be immensely helpful to Andreux in his journey."

They spent the rest of the day going over various details of the journey. Andreux was given the responsibility of leading his friends, using the map as his guide. He had to familiarize himself with every road, creek and lane on the map. Though Andreux would lead the other two, Pompompulous was the backup. He also had to remember the locations and times that they were to meet with Veritus and his messengers in the city.

Senfred was responsible for troubleshooting, questioning whether they had to choose a specific course of action or if and when they would be lost. If they had to break their journey for the night, they would all take shifts to keep vigil.

Veritus gave them each a copper seal to show the guards at the fort's check post, in order to enter the city. They would enter the city at different times; Andreux would be the first one. Once they entered the city, they would go in different directions, so that they would avoid arousing the curiosity of the guards. Then at a predetermined time, they would all gather at Religer's house in the city to determine a further course of action. Veritus would meet the young men at Religer's house.

They would start the next day, very early in the morning and had a lot of work to be done before then.

Old plans were foiled and new truces made.
Some prospects changed and some still remained.
When plans for the great war were drawn out and laid,
some fought with all their might, those nonchalant stayed.

"How are we ever going to get out of this rut? Nevius was our one hope. Now that he's gone, we're back to where we were, our lives and existence mean nothing." Glimp sighed. He was sitting under a tree, near the disciples' chamber, which was hidden in darkness.

"No need to be so dramatic," said Gruber. "When one door closes, many more will open. You just need to be patient."

Nevius's absence was felt most by Glimp, who now had a lot of free time to nurture his alter ego, Gruber. They were *both* glad that they did not have to be a part of his schemes anymore. At the same time, they missed Nevius because they truly felt that he was their only chance of release from poverty. They were caught between relief and sorrow.

"Remember the time he tried to get Andreux drowned in swimming lessons? If we hadn't pretended to drown ourselves to divert everyone's attention, he would've been found out long ago," said Gruber.

"It was you then? I never knew! Do you think we should've revealed his manifesto long ago?" asked Glimp.

"What has happened has happened. The way everything turned out, we're better off than if we had outed him. I think this was the best option for us," said Gruber.

"In a way, I'm relieved. Ever since the first time I helped him plant wild-cactus thorns in Andreux's bed, my hands have been tied. He always reminded me of that, whenever I got cold feet. Sometimes I wonder what would have happened if Nevius had not been caught red-handed?" said Glimp. Just then there was a whisper from behind followed by a sudden movement.

"Traitor!" Nevius pulled Glimp back with his hands.

Glimp jumped in fright. Nevius signalled him to be quiet.

"What are you doing here? If the master finds you, he will feed you to the half-world creatures," Glimp asked.

"Don't you think I know that?" said Nevius as he looked around. He dragged Glimp into a dark spot so that they would not be visible to anyone nearby. "But I was waiting for you to bring me some food. When you didn't show up, I came looking for you. We had a deal, remember?" He glared at Glimp.

"Sorry, but I just can't steal food anymore. What with the cook complaining to the master and Andreux guarding the kitchen, it's extremely difficult, almost impossible," explained Glimp.

"You are full of excuses. I should just get rid of you. As a matter of fact, I may not need your services anymore, now that I'm heading back to my father's house."

"How do you plan to go back, all by yourself? The forest is full of half-world creatures!"

"Not anymore. I've heard the master saying that he's cleansed the forest. It's now as safe as the tutelage itself," Nevius said matter-of-factly.

This statement piqued Glimp's interest. "When did you hear that? What else did you hear?"

"As you know, I've been roaming in the nearby woods, waiting for my chance to get back at Andreux. You promised to bring me food every day, in exchange for a better life for you beyond the tutelage. But, as you have managed to skip out on your promise for the past two days—" Glimp tried to protest at this accusation, but Nevius cut him off.

"As I was saying, since you have managed to skip your promise for the past two days, I was overcome with hunger and I had to risk entering the tutelage. As luck would have it, I heard Pompompulous address Andreux's mother as Queen Minerva. I decided to find out more. I hid behind a wall of the master's chamber, and put my ear on the wall to listen to the conversation, out of the sight of passers-by." He paused.

"What did you hear?" Glimp asked excitedly.

"This tutelage is harbouring fugitives. Andreux is the son of Reganor, the dead king, and his mother is the ex-queen. Senfred is the ex-minister's son. King Nefarius has offered a hefty sum of money for their heads. I'm going to the city to reveal their whereabouts and collect the reward from the king. I'll make my detailed plans tomorrow and leave the day after." As if it was an afterthought, he added, "I might consider taking you with me, if you swear allegiance to me and me alone. You have one day to make up your mind."

Having said that, Nevius walked back to his dwelling to sleep. The master's chamber opened just as he disappeared into the darkness. Glimp, afraid he might attract the attention and wrath of passers-by if they saw him with Nevius, remained in the darkness. Just when he decided to step out of darkness, the chamber door opened and out stepped Arianne and the ex-minister. Glimp stepped back into darkness again and waited till he was alone with Gruber again.

After he was sure that the others had gone, Glimp asked Gruber, "What do you think we should do? The time has to come for us to pick a side."

"I'm not sure it's that time yet, my friend. Though Pompompulous had warned us earlier that the judgement day is upon us, and now Nevius, I think we still need to keep our options open. Don't you think so?"

"I sure would like to keep my options open. But how do you think we can do that? Tomorrow, we have to either go with Nevius or stay back here. If we choose one, we will have to forego the other."

"We have all night to make up our mind," said Gruber. They slowly walked back to the chamber.

Glimp and Gruber spent the next day avoiding everyone else. They could not decide what they should do. They were not able to approach Andreux and did not know if Nevius managed to find out anything more. Finally as the day came to an end, Gruber, through Glimp, obtained limited insight into Andreux's plans for the next day. He was sure of what Nevius would do. He was not sure of his own plans, and that bothered him. He, who always had a solution ready for each and every problem, had none this time. The more he thought about it, the more confused he became. Glimp, who normally slept like a log through the night, tossed and turned in bed all night. He almost gave up all hope of getting an answer; and then it happened. The solution presented itself to him in all its glory. There it was, the most simplistic and effective answer. In fact, it was so simple that he laughed it off, because it seemed too good to be true. But it was true. And when he realized that it was *the* solution, his mind relaxed, and he dozed off.

When Gruber woke up the next day, he was not alone. He had his idea with him. The idea was so authentic; it filled him inside out, so much that he felt stuck to it. Though it was pitch dark outside and the sun was nowhere to be seen, he wanted to get out of bed. Glimp was, however, still happily snoring. The snore sounded like a song being played on a huge trumpet. Gruber did not bother waking him up properly. He just yelled in his ear, "Wake up, you snort! It's time to go!"

Glimp woke up with a start and almost jumped out of his bed. However, his body was not yet fully alert, and he managed to fall flat on the floor. As he pulled himself up, Gruber gently whispered in his ears. "We need to get ready, because I have a plan."

"What is it?" asked Glimp groggily.

"Trust me, this one'll work—if you hurry up."

"What's the rush?" asked Glimp. He was still sleepy and his eyes were half shut.

"We need to get ready, so that we can go with Andreux and company."

"What! Have you decided to switch sides?"

"Not yet. In fact, by going with him, we can keep our options open."

"What options?"

"We need to get out of the rut. We thought Nevius was our saviour, but it turns out that Andreux is the prince in exile. So if he happens to reclaim the throne, then wouldn't it be smart to be on his side?"

"So what are you trying to tell me?" Glimp raised his voice. He was even more confused and wished Gruber would stop getting ideas.

"Can't you see? It's so simple. We'll secretly meet Nevius and tell him that we will accompany Andreux."

"You must've gone twitter-brained, because that'll surely get our heads chopped off!" exclaimed Glimp.

"Can you calm down and listen to my plan, without interrupting me so many times!" Gruber sneered. He could not control his rising temper anymore. Glimp became quiet. Gruber continued describing his plan.

"We will—rather *you will* tell Nevius that we will accompany Andreux, but not because we have switched our loyalties. Tell him that we will try to slow them down and give Nevius enough lead time to reach Vauns early enough to warn the guards."

"That sounds risky. What if the guards actually capture Andreux and kill him?" Glimp was uncomfortable with his friend's idea. How he wished Gruber's brain would stop functioning and stop churning out these stinking plans! Yet he was morbidly fascinated by its likely outcome.

"With our master and the ex-minister by his side, I'm sure Andreux is bound to win this war. We need to make sure we're with him. More importantly, we need him to know that we're with him and not with Nevius. We'll only slow him down when needed, so that no one will ever doubt us."

"But why can't we remain in the tutelage, proclaim our allegiance to both Nevius and Andreux, and wait to see who emerges the victor? Why do we have to pick sides now?" Glimp asked.

"Because we need to prove our allegiance, not just proclaim it. Now enough of the talking! Let's pack. You go and convince Nevius. Take him some food and pretend that Mandrill is on your trail and that you need to hurry back. You will also need to talk to Andreux and seek our master's permission," said Gruber.

"What are we going to tell him?" asked Glimp.

"That we'd like to go with Andreux and help him in his mission."

"But nobody knows the secret yet. How will I explain that?"

"Good question, for a change! You'll tell him that you saw Pompompulous address the queen. Any more questions?"

"Why should I talk to Nevius? It's your plan," complained Glimp.

"Because he cannot see me, you fool! I will do the talking through you. Now let us go." said Gruber. He cleared his throat. "There's not much to dealing with Nevius. With Andreux, however, there is a lot of convincing to do," he said.

Glimp was not completely convinced. He packed his belongings and reluctantly trudged to meet Nevius.

When Glimp reached Nevius's hideout, he found Nevius sitting on a huge boulder under a tree, tapping his feet impatiently.

"Not a good sign," murmured Glimp to himself.

Nevius saw him approaching and a frown appeared on his face. "What took you so long, snail-feet? And what happened to my food, you half-wit?" sneered Nevius.

"Shhhh!" said Glimp, with his index finger on his nose. He looked both ways and behind him as if someone were following him. Nevius became quiet. He got up from the boulder and stepped back behind the tree. Glimp tried hard not to chuckle. Gruber was right. He could tackle Nevius. All of a sudden, Glimp believed in his friend's plan. He even felt sorry for suspecting it initially. He looked around one more time before he talked to Nevius.

"It's okay. I saw Mandrill following me and did not want to get you into any trouble." He looked around one more time, then pulled out a package from his bag and gave it to Nevius. "Here take it."

"What is it?" asked Nevius, still hiding behind the tree.

"It's food for you. I can't come with you. I would be more of a burden to you than help."

"That's true. But are you telling me the truth?"

"Of course. In fact, I'll help you by following you with Andreux and company." Glimp found it extremely hard to let these words out of his mouth.

"What?" Nevius's hand went to his sword.

Glimp trembled with fear. It took him a monnet or two to regain composure. "Listen. I'll try to delay Andreux so that you'll have enough lead time."

Nevius thought for some time, but Gruber assured Glimp that Nevius would not find anything wrong with what Glimp said.

"Well. Then I have to start, don't I? You better get back to the tutelage before anyone sees us," Nevius said. Glimp was relieved that

Nevius did not suspect a thing. He started to walk back quickly. Nevius called him back.

"Glimp. One more thing," he said.

Glimp turned back to face him. "What?"

Nevius approached him and shook his hand. "Thank you for all your help and support. It means a lot to me." He sounded sincere. For a monnet, Glimp felt guilty that he was not being honest with Nevius. However, that guilt quickly passed when he remembered how Nevius always ridiculed and belittled him. He looked at Nevius, smiled and walked back towards the tutelage. He had taken a few more steps when Nevius called him again.

"If I think I'm slowing down, I'll leave heaps of brown twigs on the ground for your attention. If I get sleepy, I'll leave three rocks of same size and shape on the right side of the path. Watch out for these signs." And with that, Nevius ran out of sight.

Glimp found the master talking to Andreux and Senfred. It took him a while to convince Hermitus in allowing him to accompany Andreux and others. When Hermitus consented, Glimp was genuinely happy.

They soon joined the departing group. Glimp looked at Andreux and Senfred. "When do we leave?"

"As soon as Pompompulous joins us," said Senfred.

"And here I am." Glimp heard Pompompulous's voice behind him. He had a huge bag tied to his back.

"What all did you pack in your bag, 'Pulous?" asked Senfred.

"Must be food!" Glimp did not have any doubt whatsoever about that.

"It's not food that I carry with me, you hungry mongrel," quipped Pompompulous. He emptied the bag and showed the contents to his friends. It was an amazing assortment of tools and medicines. There were medicines for all sorts of sickness and antidotes for almost all sorts of poisons. Then there were a few gaze-crystals, to view far and near, and some glare-crystals, which shed light in darkness. They were wrapped in a cloth bag that also contained instructions for the crystals' use.

"This is so cool!" Glimp wanted to hold it, but Pompompulous put it back in the bag.

Also among the contents of Pompompulous's bag was a small pickaxe to cut branches and twigs that would hinder their way. There were some pebbles, coins, sticks of various shapes and sizes, pouches filled with water, weird-looking rocks with illegible writings on them, and Pompompulous's clothes and bedroll to sleep during the night time.

"Wow!" exclaimed Glimp.

"No wonder it took you some time to pack," said Andreux as he helped Pompompulous put the bag on his back. "Thank you for your foresight. Who knows, we might need all of it."

Pompompulous smiled. He then looked at Glimp, "And about the food that you mentioned. Since my bag is full, you need to carry the food." Glimp did not protest. He wanted to look eager to be with them. And after all, if the bag felt too heavy, he could always eat some food.

PART TWO

IN THE FOREST

Chapter Eight
The Journey Begins

Friendship and loyalty are traits of virtue.
Words do not count until actions see them through.
Keep your word, no matter how hard it is to.
Treat your friend just as you like him to treat you.

Andreux and Senfred took the blessings of Minerva, Veritus and Hermitus when it was time to leave. Veritus stepped towards Senfred, looked at him with great affection and hugged him.

"I'll make you proud of me, father," said Senfred.

"I'm sure of that, Senfred."

Hermitus reminded Andreux, "Always keep the map with you. Never lose it, because that will give away our plans. When you step into the forest, watch out for the first black birch tree, it is marked on the map with a black circle. You must take the path to its left. After you walk for about seven *megallids*[11], you will pass the first checkpoint, a banyan tree. This is different from any other tree in the vicinity. The prop roots of the tree have been sculpted out of stone by an anonymous sculptor and placed there. It is believed that the guardian forces of the forest reside there.

"You can choose to rest there for the night, but I advise you to continue on until you reach the riverbed. Sojourn there for the night. The river bed is another four megallids from the banyan tree.

"While you are travelling towards the riverbed, you will go past a dilapidated shelter. It was used as a spy post in the past by Nefarius, but it has been unoccupied for some time. Rumour has it that an ogress lives there, so I caution you not to stop.

"Once you continue with your journey the next day, it will not be long before you reach the Capirona. From then on, follow the instructions inscribed on the map.

11   seven megallids are approximately equivalent to thirty miles

"Also remember to meet Veritus at the chosen spot at the decided time, at any cost. Timing is crucial for the plan to work."

"I'll remember, Master," Andreux replied.

"May the forces of nature be with you and make your journey free of obstacles," Minerva said.

Thus the friends set out on foot, with bags on their backs and hopes in their hearts.

Andreux looked back and waved to his mother before finally disappearing into the jungle. He opened the map and took a quick glance. He needed to find a black birch tree to determine which way they went. He looked ahead for the path that would ultimately lead them to Vauns. When he found the black birch tree, his face lit up.

"This way," he said. The walk into the jungle was not too bad. There was still a lot of light. The gentle sounds of the river flowing nearby on the rocks were cheerful. "It's important to stay together. Though the master has freed the forest of the half-world creatures, he wanted us to be careful. We do not know what dangers may lie ahead."

"Wise words," commented Pompompulous. His gaze fell on Senfred, who seemed to be lost in his thoughts. He gently nudged him in the elbow. "What are you thinking about?" he asked him.

"I was just thinking about how our lives changed forever in one night. We were blissfully unaware for all these yedibs and now here we are, on this mighty journey to find our destiny," said Senfred.

"So true. It seems like a fairy tale," said Glimp.

"Except it's not. It's time to set things right and make sure that this story has a happy ending," said Pompompulous.

Andreux, who was leading by a few footsteps, motioned his friends to stop.

"Listen," said Andreux. "Can you hear that?" They could hear faint sounds a little far away; sounds of what could be footsteps crushing dried leaves on the ground. Glimp looked around and noticed heaps of dried brown twigs.

"I can't hear anything," Glimp said, "All I hear is stomachs rumbling for food." He almost immediately sat down on a nearby rock and put his bag over the twig heap.

"We have a long way to travel," protested Pompompulous.

"Which is even more reason for us to be strong and agile. Why don't you have a quick bite and we can resume our journey," said Glimp as he sat down. Senfred looked questioningly at Glimp.

"What?" asked Glimp.

"Nothing. I can understand if anyone else is hungry. But the cook said that you took food from the kitchen this morning. So why are you so eager for a bite?" he asked. Glimp was caught in a dilemma, but Gruber came to his rescue.

"You don't know me at all. I am a good friend, just trying to support you. I never said I would eat now, did I? I should tell you about the time when I—" He was interrupted by Andreux.

"I'm sure we'll have a lot of time to get to know one another better. We have a long way ahead of us. So why don't those of us who are hungry have some food? We can talk when we resume walking. We need to get to a safe resting place before it gets dark, and for that we do not have the luxury of slowing down."

When they resumed walking after a light snack, Pompompulous took the pickaxe from his bag and held it in his hand.

"What's that for?" asked Glimp.

"The forest is becoming dense. Very soon, we'll need to clear the way," he explained. Then he noticed a rough path lay ahead of them, branches cut and shrubs uprooted and thrown aside.

"I wonder ..." He stared ahead.

"But if the forest gets dense, then don't we have to worry about the wild beasts that wander here? I'm sure that would be a greater challenge than watching out for branches and twigs," said Glimp.

"If we stay together as one, then we don't have to fear the wild animals. As long as we don't willingly disturb their peace, we'll be safe from their attacks," said Senfred.

"But what about Pompompulous? He's afraid of wild animals," Glimp cried out.

"I think I'll be all right," said Pompompulous.

"What happened when you went looking for the stranger, Pompompulous? I bet you were terrified, weren't you?" asked Glimp.

"I was a little afraid," confessed Pompompulous. But then Senfred came to his rescue.

"But that did not stop him then and it will not stop him now. We will all take care of him. As you said earlier, 'Pulous, you are a good friend to have. We're thankful that you are here and we'll make sure that you don't get hurt."

Everyone fell silent for a few monnets.

Then Pompompulous spoke. "I don't want to become a nuisance to you. I'd rather go back to tutelage now, before it is too late."

Andreux requested that he stay with them. If he really became scared, then he could go back at that time. Pompompulous reluctantly agreed. Glimp was so caught up in the conversation that he asked, without thinking, "How can he go back by himself then? I'm sure he will be afraid to return by himself."

"I'm sure you wouldn't mind going back with him. Andreux and I have to go. It is our destiny. No one else is bound to it," said Senfred.

Everyone became quiet.

Very soon, Andreux also noticed fallen branches and crushed leaves. He looked around to see if someone was nearby. Glimp had apparently realized that he couldn't keep changing the topic forever, so he remained silent.

"Whoever it is, they've made our lives easier," Senfred remarked.

"I'm wary of blindly following someone else's tracks," replied Pompompulous.

"You are afraid that it might be an animal," Glimp teased.

"That wasn't a very nice thing to say, Glimp," Senfred scolded.

"But it's not as if our path has been cleared completely; we still have quite a few obstacles in our way," Glimp remarked.

"That's true. I guess as long as we're on the right track, we need not worry about following someone. And we aren't even sure if there is someone at all." Andreux referred to the map. They were still on the path marked out on it. Soon the forest became so dense that the trees blocked all sunlight. It was not sundown yet, but it was hard to see. The path became narrow and the ground was covered with sharp rocks and thorny bushes. Pompompulous removed a glare-crystal and gave it to Andreux. The crystal emitted a dim light, barely enough to show the path a few footsteps ahead. No sooner than Pompompulous pulled out the glare-crystal from his bag, two twinkling lights appeared farther away. One was green and the other was blue. "Are those the eyes of a beast?" asked Glimp.

"No. They're lumen-drobs. Remember what Master taught us about them at tutelage?" replied Pompompulous.

"The mischief mongers!" cried Glimp.

"Shh," said Senfred.

Hermitus had taught them that lumen-drobs were magical creatures of the forest who were quite powerful. They were as small as tiny sparks of light, yet their magic could harm an entire kingdom. The lumen-drobs came in different colours, depending on their lineage. There were hundreds of types of lumen-drobs, and they only stayed in forests. Hermitus had taught them not to attract their attention. Andreux did not want the lumen-drobs to interrupt their plans.

The four friends continued cautiously along the path together. Andreux had only one goal in mind. He had to reach a resting place before sundown. He had three places to choose from, depending upon how fast or slow the group was. First there was a dilapidated shelter. His master had cautioned him to check for inhabitants or any signs of occupancy before preparing to spend the night there. Spies of Nefarius had used that shelter several hogashes ago to keep track of suspicious activities happening in Aranya. The next alternative would be the riverside, which was quite a distance from the shelter. But there would be enough moonlight, and this was by far the safest place. One of them would have to remain awake and keep vigil. Everyone would take turns so that no one would get tired. The third alternative was the ruined temple, if they managed to get there in time. But they were warned by their master not to stay there.

"I wonder why the riverbed is safe, when we know that there are more creatures underwater than there are on ground?" said Andreux.

"Well the only threat at the riverside is from wildlife. Though the river has many magical creatures, this particular place is free of them all. An Atttymine king cleansed his kingdom of all magical creatures. The riverside shared borders with Attyme and consequently is safe for the night halt," replied Pompompulous.

As the forest grew denser, it became more and more difficult for the young men to stay together. Frequently, one of them would accidentally wander onto an obscure path as if pulled by unseen forces. The glow from the glare-crystal was not enough for all of them. Unfortunately, Pompompulous could only find one in his bag. So if one of the group felt sleepy or tired or if his mind wandered off, he would get a little behind and manage to get lost in the darkness that surrounded them. But Andreux and Senfred were vigilant. This slowed the group a little bit. Noticing this, Glimp managed to wander away from the group every now and then to slow them down more.

When Glimp lagged behind again, Pompompulous about called him on it. "It almost seems like you want to get lost and slow us down."

"That's not fair. And I'm sorry if my clumsiness is causing you all so much grief." Glimp pretended to be upset.

"Please don't fight over such small issues. We need to reach our destination before night is upon us," said Andreux.

"Let me sing then," offered Glimp. "That will keep us alert and you'll all know that I'm with you." And without waiting to hear the protests of Senfred or Pompompulous, he started to sing:

> When we are together, we are not lost
> In the blazing sun or ice-cold frost
> tra la la … tri li li … we are not lost.
> We are not lost, we are not lost.

Before Glimp could continue with his song, Pompompulous grabbed him and clamped his hands over Glimp's mouth.

"You're going to wake up the wildlife, you fool. Be quiet," he whispered harshly. Just then Andreux stopped dead in his tracks. Everyone looked to see what the matter was.

Ahead of them was the mammoth, standing tall and mighty on its four legs. Steam was gushing out of its nostrils. Its horns were sharp and heavy, shining off the glare from its blood-red eyes. Its mane was covered with thick, black, curled fur. Giant tusks protruded from either side of its mouth. When it stood, it was twice as tall as Andreux and three times as thick as all of them put together. It was looking keenly at Andreux.

Mammoths and monsters, enormous, colossal
Their natures are undisguised, intentions real.
But as creatures of pride, conceit, slander and evil,
humans cause more damage, put lives in peril.

"Great heavens!" exclaimed Senfred, looking at the mammoth. As the mammoth stared at them without batting an eyelid, Andreux, though he had never witnessed a beast of this size and massive proportions, held his gaze steady.

Pompompulous let go of Glimp when he saw the mammoth. He took a few steps back, overcome with immense fear. Glimp stepped back instinctively. As soon as the mammoth saw the men retreat, it stepped forward.

Andreux addressed his companions but maintained eye contact with the mammoth. "Don't move away. The mammoth can sense fear. So regain composure. We all need to stay together."

Gruber was the first to react to Andreux's words. He pulled Glimp along with him, stepped forward and stood next to Senfred. Glimp could not immediately look at the mammoth.

"I'm scared," he said.

"No need to be scared. Muster up some courage," Andreux said. Finally, Glimp lifted his head high to look at the beast. "I'd turn into an instant fossil, if it ever decided to trample upon me. What a huge beast it is. I hope I live long enough to tell this story to my grandchildren!"

Pompompulous was the last to join them. His fear of animals came in like a flood. If he was scared for his life when he saw the snake in his master's chamber, this was a million times worse. He felt as if his life was being sucked out of him. His face paled to a ghostly white and his entire body trembled.

Fortunately Senfred came to his rescue. "Come on 'Pulous. Stand in between me and Andreux," he offered, taking Pompompulous's hand and gently pulling him forward. Pompompulous took his time. His head remained lowered. His shivering subsided, however.

Senfred pushed up Pompompulous's chin, keeping his eye contact with the mammoth. When the beast perceived fear in the eyes of Pompompulous, it roared mightily. The sound reminded Pompompulous of a mighty thunderstorm. Steam gushed out of the animal's nostrils.

"Now regain your composure. The worst thing you can do is let the beast suspect that you're afraid of it," said Senfred. "You know that 'Pulous, don't you?"

Pompompulous felt ashamed. Of course he knew that. He had been so overcome with mortal fear that he remembered nothing for that short span in time. Memory meant nothing without courage and conviction, he realized. "Thank you, Senfred. I also remember that Master taught us once that a mammoth is not afraid of anything except fire," he said.

"Excellent. All of you maintain eye contact with the beast. It's slow to react. I'll light the torch," said Andreux. He took the torch from his bag and two flame-stones, which he rubbed against one another. A tiny spark erupted from the stones and he quickly used it to light his torch. He passed it to Senfred, who used it to light his own torch. Senfred then passed it on to Pompompulous. Soon everyone had their torches lit. On the count of three, they all brought out their torches in front of them. The fire from the torches danced fiercely in the beast's eyes.

There was an immense commotion as the mammoth gave out another roar. It trampled the ground on which it stood. Andreux shoved his torch closer to the beast. The beast retaliated and stepped towards them.

"Careful now, Andreux. Don't get it too excited," Senfred said. The friends stood frozen, with torches in their hands. The mammoth stood still as well. Only this time, it was not mighty; it looked afraid. It stepped back slowly, its gaze still on the intruders. The young men watched the monstrous animal disappear into darkness.

"Let's keep the torches lit until we are safe from its reach," suggested Andreux.

"I completely forgot about the torches," said Glimp. "Why were we not using them to guide us in the dark?"

"The torches don't last long, and we don't have more than one each. We really need to save them for emergencies such as these," said Andreux.

"That was close," sighed Glimp. "I didn't think I would make it."

Senfred, noticing that Pompompulous was unusually silent, asked, "What is it 'Pulous?" Pompompulous did not say anything.

"He must still be in a state of shock," Glimp remarked.

"I wasn't prepared for that. I could've easily died without the mammoth having to take one step towards me," said Pompompulous. His voice was meek.

"But that's how such encounters are, my friend. They do not come with prior notice." said Glimp.

Senfred spoke. "The most important thing is that we've overcome the obstacle. And he has overcome his fear when it really mattered. And I'm sure he will again, if required."

At that very instant, Glimp yelled "I sssssee a sssssnake!" and collapsed on the ground, as if he fainted. Pompompulous jumped in fright, beads of sweat covering his forehead.

"Where is it?" Andreux looked everywhere.

"I think he mistook this for a snake," said Senfred, pointing to a prop root hanging from a nearby tree.

"He must've been a bundle of nerves after seeing the mammoth," said Andreux as Senfred sprinkled some water on Glimp's face to revive him. Glimp opened his eyes, looked around and stood up. He almost lost his balance, but Pompompulous caught him just in time.

"Maybe it's not such a good idea that Glimp and I continue slowing you down," said Pompompulous. "It may be better if we go back."

Glimp dismissed the idea. "We all have our weaknesses. That doesn't mean we are unfit to help our friends!" he exclaimed. "Moreover, we have almost reached the destination for tonight, haven't we Andreux?"

Andreux carefully examined the tree and its prop roots.

"It certainly is the banyan tree that our master told us to watch for!" he exclaimed. "Look at the intricate carvings on these stone props!"

Everyone gathered to take a closer look. They looked like real prop roots, yet they were made of stone and were carved with snakes that intertwined throughout the length of the roots. They also had inscriptions in a script that was unknown to the group.

"We're certainly on the right path. We must be getting closer to the ruined shelter," said Andreux.

"We've come this far. Let us stay with you. It means a lot that you have agreed to take us with you on this important journey," requested Glimp, in his gruff voice.

"But ..." Pompompulous protested.

"He's right 'Pulous. You don't know how much your company means to us. Don't be upset by these occurrences. We'll certainly need your help once we reach Vauns. You know the place better than us," said Senfred.

"I'll agree on one condition," said Pompompulous.

"What's that?" asked Andreux.

"If another incident occurs, the two of us return to the tutelage. There will be no more discussions at that time. And that is final," he said. "I have made up my mind. I very much desire to accompany you, but I also desire for you to accomplish your mission without any setbacks. After all, Master had warned you that time is important for your plans to succeed."

"Sounds fair enough to me," said Andreux.

"I suppose the setback should relate to animals," said Glimp, smirking. The smirk did not escape the attentive eye of Pompompulous.

"What are you smirking for?" he asked. Glimp became quiet after that.

"Let us not get caught up in this squabbling," Andreux cautioned them as he led the way. After quite some time, Andreux looked at the ground and exclaimed, "Look. I see some freshly made footprints. Someone must have passed this way recently. Whoever it is, we must be very close to them. Let us be careful and prepared, just in case there is danger ahead."

Life's full of twists and turns, surprises galore.
Expect the unexpected; to come there's always more.
If you cross paths with lumen-drobs, I implore
cheer them, befriend them, lest you feel their furor.

Although Glimp remained quiet, Pompompulous wondered if he was up to something. His mind raced back to everything that had happened that day. When he reviewed the facts, he found there was a pattern in Glimp's behaviour.

He remembered that before they left the tutelage, the cook had told him that Glimp went to have food. Later when Glimp decided to stop to eat, he had sat down almost immediately. Chances were that he did not eat anything. Then what was Glimp doing? He had come back with his bag from the kitchen. Now why would he carry the bag all the way to kitchen and then come back with it? He could have just left it with someone else, unless he needed the bag for some reason. Why would he need the bag?

Pompompulous also recollected Glimp uttering something about twig heaps and rock piles. Was that a code of sorts? If yes, what could that be? It then struck him that when they stopped the first time, Glimp had put his bag on a heap of brown twigs. Was that a coincidence? Or did he have a silly idea to stop whenever they came across a twig heap? No, it was not to be dismissed so lightly, he thought. Could it have anything to do with Nevius? The idea seemed improbable. Would Nevius be following them? Or were they, in fact, following him? How did he get involved? Glimp had, after all, been Nevius's close aide. Maybe he was wrong in judging, but he could not trust Glimp anymore. He decided to keep an eye on him from then on.

Glimp and Gruber, for their part, became very careful. They did not want to arouse anyone's suspicions. Even more, they did not want to go back with Pompompulous. So there were no more tricks to hinder their speed. Gruber's heart skipped a beat. They must be catching up with Nevius. After all, Nevius was accustomed to a life of luxury; surely he could not walk as fast as the forest-bred, Gruber thought. And to add to that, Nevius had to clear the way, whereas they did not have to. Glimp wiped the sweat from his brow.

It was soon time for sundown. Pompompulous noted that they might need another glare-crystal, so he looked in his bag, just in case he had more.

When Pompompulous was busy looking for another glare-crystal, Gruber signalled to Glimp. Glimp looked at him enquiringly.

Gruber closed his eyes, as if he felt sleepy. He yawned a little.

Glimp understood the clue and pulled out a little bottle from his bag. It was an ordinary-looking bottle that could be held in a young man's palm with just the lid showing. Inside, it had a dark purplish potion that gave out an odourless gas. On the bottle was a small label that read "sleep-inducing potion."

The potion was one of the tools that Glimp had managed to pack; he'd thought it might come in handy to slow them down. Because the gas would cause sleep almost instantaneously, he had shut the lid tightly. Glimp found it extremely annoying to open the tightly wound lid.

"Why would anyone want to—" he started aloud, alerting Pompompulous.

"Why would anyone do what, Glimp?" Pompompulous asked him, managing to pull out the glare-crystal and close his bag. He gave the crystal to Senfred, who was walking a few steps ahead of him.

"I think we're getting close to the first halt, the dilapidated shelter," exclaimed Andreux as he studied the map.

Glimp managed to put the bottle back in his bag without Pompompulous noticing.

"Are we breaking the journey here for the night?" asked Glimp. If they did, then he did not have to use any more tricks.

To Glimp's dismay, Andreux replied, "No. If we continue at the same rate for some more time, we'll reach the riverside soon. That would be my choice. What would you say, Senfred?"

"That was our master's first choice. Let us abide by that," replied Senfred.

Gruber knew that if they continued walking, they would catch up with Nevius. In spite of Glimp's plans and the unexpected delay with the mammoth, somehow the group had managed to gain momentum in their pursuit. After taking a few more steps, Gruber signalled to Glimp to use the potion. Just as Glimp was about to reach for the bottle in his bag, Pompompulous let out a loud cry. "Help! I think I see the mammoth again!" With that, he seemed to faint, his body dangerously leaning on Glimp as if he were falling on him.

Taken aback, Glimp managed to stop himself from collapsing and tried hard to prevent Pompompulous from falling over onto him. Andreux and Senfred joined him. Pompompulous's eyes were closed.

As Senfred was busy reviving Pompompulous, Glimp panicked for a moment. He looked around to see if there was truly a mammoth nearby. He had not fully recovered from the earlier encounter. When he could not see the beast, he looked back at Gruber and was surprised to see his friend's face red with anger. He figured out what could have happened.

Glimp was furious that Pompompulous had so cleverly foiled his plan. And the end came sooner than he'd thought. He could still foresee himself telling the story of his encounter with the mammoth to his grandchildren, but he was not as rich as he had previously envisioned. He was living in a hut, and the roof was caving in. And there were flies everywhere. His grandchildren were filthy, with ragged clothes and unkempt hair. And all of this because he could not open the bottle without arousing Pompompulous's suspicion.

Pompompulous appeared to revive with Senfred's attempts. He smiled weakly and apologized to Andreux for delaying their journey one more time. But this was it, he said. He was returning to tutelage, but he needed company. He pretended to limp. Glimp resisted vehemently, but it was of no use.

"Maybe Pompompulous is right. Maybe this journey is destined for us alone," said Senfred.

Glimp protested, but Andreux had the final word. "It is our mission, and maybe it is destined that only we are supposed to be on it. I can't afford to lose any more time. I sincerely appreciate your gesture to accompany us, but I'll have to take you up on your offer some other time."

The group split at that point. Andreux and Senfred moved ahead. Pompompulous let them have his glare-crystals. Glimp objected to it.

"We need one for ourselves too," he said.

"But I only have two. And we are in no rush to get back to tutelage, are we? We can travel when it's daylight and rest when it's dark."

Glimp's fury was about to erupt, but he grudgingly followed Pompompulous.

Earlier, when Pompompulous had cautioned his friends about lumen-drobs, the lumen-drobs had heard Glimp's comments. They had waited for the group to get ahead, and after the young men walked farther away, they had followed them.

"Us, mischief mongers, they called!" said one to another.

"If mischief is what they want, cause mischief we will," said the other.

The two lumen-drobs were now following Glimp, Pompompulous and Gruber, who was visible to their powerful vision.

"The red-face!" said the blue lumen-drob, pointing to Gruber. "More mischief he does than we."

"And yet," said the green lumen-drob, "we the mischief-mongers are!"

"What have we for them?" asked the blue one. The second one pulled a wand out from under its wing. The wand was small, almost the size of an ant's leg. Waving the wand, it sang thus:

The cat is out of the bag.
This trip comes to a snag.

Into foes turn these friends,
and that is how it ends.

While the blue lumen-drob chanted the spell again, the green one sprinkled some dust into the air. Then the lumen-drobs disappeared.

Pompompulous was the first one to react to the spell. He stopped walking abruptly and turned to Glimp. "I've seen through your act. Why did you do those things?"

Glimp was startled. "What act? What are you talking about?" he asked innocently.

"Don't try those tricks with me, Glimp. I've seen everything from the heap-twigs to the sleeping potion. Why did you do it?"

By that time, Glimp was under the influence of the magic as well.

"If you've seen everything, you should've figured it out by now," said Gruber. He was fully in control of Glimp's body and continued without waiting for Pompompulous to reply. "I was this close to having my way. You had to interfere! Always playing the sacrificing, intelligent martyr!"

Pompompulous was taken aback. "I didn't know you felt so strongly, Glimp!"

"If I did, why would you care? After all, you are the son of Prosperus. You don't need to mingle with us wretched, poor folk once you are back in the city. You'll go back and become a merchant of some sorts. Your life is all cut-out for you. It isn't for us. We need to think hogashes ahead for every little thing we do," Gruber went on.

"That isn't true. I've never treated you less because you were poor," Pompompulous objected.

"Then why would you not trust us? Why do you have to constantly keep vigil? Why, Pompompulous?" Gruber's voice sounded menacing and dangerous.

"My distrust has nothing to do with your economic status, you fool. I distrust you because you are in league with Nevius."

"What if we are? So what?"

"I knew it. He was here all along. He was clearing the path for us. Every time he left you a signal, you would slow us down. You've betrayed the trust my friends and I had placed in you, you ungrateful wretch!" Pompompulous shouted.

"What are you going to do about it now? You are one against two. You can't escape us!" said Gruber.

"Who is 'us'? Why do you keep referring to yourself as two people?" asked Pompompulous.

"It is because I have company that you cannot see," revealed Glimp.

"You must be out of your mind, talking like that."

"Maybe, maybe not. It doesn't matter now, does it Gruber?" asked Glimp.

"Who is Gruber?" Pompompulous became cautious.

"It's me, you fool!" Glimp's vicious voice echoed in darkness "Come on, let us get him." He turned his head to talk to Gruber.

"You don't mean that, Glimp. Don't do anything that you'll regret," said Pompompulous.

But it was too late. Gruber and, under his influence, Glimp pounced upon Pompompulous. Even though Glimp was no match for his size, he gained the upper hand by attacking Pompompulous from both sides. Pompompulous stood his ground as best he could, hitting Glimp with his fists and kicking with his legs, using all his brute force. But he was no match for a possessed person, and Glimp poured his anger at all the unfortunate circumstances in his life out onto the person in his grasp.

They were both hurt. With cheeks swollen, hands bruised, clothes ripped and bleeding eyes, it was a ghastly sight. Finally Pompompulous could not fight any more. He fell to the ground with a big thud. It was then that Glimp and Gruber realized the enormity of what they had done. By then the effect of the magic was wearing off. But the anger was still present.

"What do we do now?" asked Glimp.

"Let's tie him up and give him the sleeping potion. That'll keep him drugged for some time," said Gruber.

"What happens when he wakes up?" asked Glimp again. Gruber looked around. It was dark. Glimp fumbled with his bag and pulled out his torch. He lit it and looked around.

"There seems to be a cave there. Let's dump his body inside and close it with a big rock or something," he suggested. It was not an easy task. Pompompulous was fairly heavy and Glimp and Gruber were tired after the fight. However, Glimp managed to tie Pompompulous up and give him the sleeping potion, closing his own nose so that he would not fall asleep.

Then, with great difficulty, he dragged Pompompulous's body to the cave. After he finally shoved Pompompulous's body into the cave, he pulled a few large rocks and tree barks in front to cover it up. When he was done, he sighed and sat down. He was not sure if Pompompulous was dead or alive.

"What next, Gruber?" asked Glimp.

"Maybe we should go back and tell Andreux that Pompompulous did not need us after all."

Glimp suddenly remembered something and looked around. "Where is our bag? And our torch?" He looked perplexed. They looked everywhere but could not find them.

"Do you want to look in the cave?" asked Glimp.

"Are you out of your mind? Let's just forget about the bags," cried Gruber.

"Then we can't go back to Andreux. Look at the mess that we are in. They'll figure out something went wrong and kill us then and there," said Glimp.

"I have an idea," said Gruber. Glimp noticed a small twinkle in his eyes. "Let's say we came across the mammoth again. Only this time Pompompulous was not as fortunate. We tried fighting it off, but the beast disappeared into the darkness with him. Now how does that sound?"

Glimp was overjoyed when he heard his friend's suggestion. Maybe all was not yet lost. "Wonderful. Then let us go find Andreux and Senfred," he said. They walked and walked and then walked some more. But there was no sight of them.

"Maybe we should run, since we must have lost considerable time in that fight," suggested Gruber. So they ran.

After some time, they stopped to catch their breath. "We've been running like madmen for some time now. It's totally dark here. And there's no trace of Andreux or Senfred." Glimp began to panic.

"Not even Nevius, for that matter," added Gruber.

"Do you think we might be lost?" asked Glimp.

"I do not know what to **think** anymore. I think we are at a dead end here." Gruber was finally stumped. Glimp was mighty tired as well. He had lost the food bag while fighting with Pompompulous. *What are we going to do now?* he wondered.

"You got us into a fine pickle. Thanks to your marvellous idea, we're now doomed, destined to live as outcasts in Aranya for the rest of our lives." Glimp was annoyed at how things had finally shaped up.

"If only you were tactful! What a stupid thing to try to use the yawning potion when Pompompulous was watching you!" yelled Gruber.

"Hey! Don't blame me. I should've never played along with your plan. I wish I had stayed at the tutelage!" There was a touch of despair in Glimp's voice.

"You should have. I knew you never had it in you to change your destiny."

Glimp accepted Gruber's words with reluctance. "I'm sorry. I shouldn't have taken it out on you like that. We're in this together," he acknowledged. He paused for breath. "Now what do we do? Where do we go from here?"

"I guess there's only one way for us now. We need go back to where we came from."

They got up and looked around. It was dark everywhere and they could not see anything.

"I think we're lost in this slimy darkness. Maybe we should wait until tomorrow," said Gruber. Just then he saw two tiny flashes of light a little farther away.

"Lumen-drobs! We must be careful," said Glimp, remembering what Pompompulous had said earlier that day.

"Let's use their light to figure out a way out of this dead end," suggested Gruber The two friends started down a familiar-looking path.

"Look at this broken birch tree. I remember seeing this," exclaimed Glimp.

"And I remember passing by these rocks before. I wondered if Nevius had anything to do with them," said Gruber after a few steps. "We must be on the right track, then." They walked slowly.

After what seemed to be a long walk, Glimp found a shiny object on the ground. He picked it up and exclaimed, "Here's a gaze-crystal from Pompompulous's bag. We must be getting closer to the cave!"

"But I thought Pompompulous gave the crystals to Andreux before parting." Gruber was not convinced with Glimp's discovery.

"Let's see if we find his bag here. Maybe he had one more in his bag, that he kept for himself. It was a big bag, after all," said Glimp.

"Maybe," said Gruber. He still had his doubts, but they walked further. They passed by a broken birch tree.

"Look. This is the broken birch tree that we … now wait a minute! Did we not just pass by this tree?"

"I think we did, Glimp. We're roaming in circles," said Gruber as they approached the rocks once again. Whatever little hope they had in their hearts disappeared now. Fear and despair crept in and caused them to shiver.

Lumen-drobs, lumen-drobs, beware ye mortals.
Let not their size fool ye, they could be ruthless
If they choose, ye be a king, or could be worthless.
Beware of lumen-drobs; beware ye mortals.

While Glimp and Gruber, lost in the dense forest without the slightest hope of finding their way out of the darkness, were partly to be blamed for the mess they were in, they were not the only cause. True, had he not listened to Gruber or had he not remained so undecided until the last moment, he might have been sleeping in his warm, comfortable bed at the tutelage. Yet the magic in the forest was beyond their control.

The tiny flickering blue and green specks of lights, which Pompompulous had correctly identified as lumen-drobs, belonged to Aranya, and, as the lumen-drobs believed, the forest belonged to them and to them alone. Any mortal interference was not tolerated. The intruders would be used for their amusement for some time and then disposed of or expelled from the forest once they tired of them.

Fortuna and Ilvila, the lumen-drobs that had caused a major detour in the plans of the group from Hermitus's tutelage, dwelled in the central part of Aranya. Fortuna showered the passers-by with good luck, and Ilvila, bad luck. Together, they created mischief with magic. That day, it so happened that Fortuna had decided to help Andreux, but Ilvila wanted to fill his path with various obstacles.

Fortuna, the green lumen-drob, had her hair decked with tiny precious gems. She wore garments that shone like silk but were made of a rare material that was not found on Earth. Her tiny wings flapped noiselessly as she waved her wand at the tired friends, who quickly slipped into a deep slumber.

Ilvila, the blue lumen-drob was very untidy and was dressed in rags. Her wand was cracked and twisted as if it had been trampled upon by a herd of elephants and handed down several generations. She twitched her nose impatiently while her friend cast magic.

Fortuna looked at the lost friends. She pitied them. "Alas! The mysterious ways of human nature! Not many mortals resist fame and fortune; they are easily tempted. Has a weakness, the strongest warrior."

Ilvila smiled. "Such weaknesses, we feast on. It is a pleasure, to play with these, mortals full of weaknesses."

They waited until Glimp and Gruber fell asleep. Then they flew away from the spot. They rose higher and higher until they reached the topmost branch of the tallest tree in that part of the forest. They settled on the branch and looked at each other. With a quick snap of fingers, they grew in size. Soon they transformed into two fairies, slightly smaller than an average female index finger. No sooner had they transformed than they started arguing with each other.

"Why did you make the two men lose their way?" asked Ilvila.

"For the same reason that you made them attack Pompompulous!" replied Fortuna.

"I had to punish them. They should not have stepped into my realm."

"Our realm!" Fortuna corrected her. At that point, they stared hard at each other for a brief moment and burst out laughing. They laughed and danced on the branch, and as they danced the entire tree swayed dangerously back and forth. With shrill voices, they sang a song that echoed menacingly in the woods.

> We ye thee lumen-drobs, fairies of forest
> With good luck and bad luck, trespassers we subject
> Dum duma dum, dum duma dum, bells on our trumpet
> We ye thee lumen-drobs, fairies of forest.

> Welcome we, visitors to take on our test.
> The one who survives it will win our respect.
> Dum duma dum, dum duma dum, bells on our trumpet
> We ye thee lumen-drobs, fairies of forest.

Some times our mood is foul, heart filled with contempt.
We might not like it, the sound of your footstep
Dum duma dum, dum duma dum, bells on our trumpet
We ye thee lumen-drobs, fairies of forest."

Men have come; men have gone, no winner, not yet.
Those who lost, lost lives or lived to be remnants.
Dum duma dum, dum duma dum, bells on our trumpet
We ye thee lumen-drobs, fairies of forest.

"What do you want to do now?" asked Ilvila.

"I am bored with these men. They have served their purpose. The man in the cave is as good as dead and these two sleeping here are of no consequence to me anymore. Let us have some fun with the other two," said Fortuna. Thus they flew away to find Andreux and Senfred. With them went their magic.

Chapter Twelve
Bugata

Magic or malady, evil intentions
Cause is irrelevant, of no significance
What makes a difference is heartfelt repentance
Own up to your actions, face the consequence.

As soon as Fortuna and Ilvila left, Glimp and Gruber woke up from their slumber. At first, they did not know what happened. It all seemed like a dream, a bad nightmare. But when he realized what they had done to Pompompulous, Glimp was mortally scared.

"Let's run away from all this," he suggested.

"Running away is not a solution," said Gruber.

"Let's go anywhere far away. Let's live incognito from now on. We can change our names so that no one will ever know about us."

"I just said running away is not an option."

"So much for keeping our options open," muttered Glimp.

"You should've come up with a better idea then," shouted Gruber. He stopped when he caught a glimpse of fairy dust on Glimp's clothes. What else could have caused everything to go so haywire? He recollected Pompompulous warning them against lumen-drobs. It must have been *their* work! But would anyone ever believe them? The fact remained that everything that Glimp had blurted out to Pompompulous had been true. The lumen-drobs just caused it all to pour out of him, like lava out of a volcano. But there was no point in crying over spilt milk. They had to find their way out.

Glimp closed his eyes and prayed fervently for a solution. When he opened his eyes, he saw something shine on the ground, not far from where he stood. It was a feeble light, but something was shining nevertheless. He bent down and picked it up gingerly.

"What is it?" asked Gruber.

"It looks like a potion bottle. It must have slipped out of Pompompulous's bag," exclaimed Glimp as he held it in his hand. Gruber looked at it carefully. Even though it was pitch dark, the contents of the bottle were shining, emitting just enough light to read the label on the bottle.

"It is the lepana, to see in darkness," shouted Gruber in excitement. "The god must have heard your prayers." Glimp took some potion from the bottle and applied it to his eyes. The whole forest became illuminated and now they could see everything, as if it were bright and sunny.

"Maybe we should go back to the cave to see if Pompompulous is still alive," suggested Glimp. He felt remorse for what they had done to him.

"I'm not sure that will help. We need outside help now. Let's leave the forest as quickly as we can. Hopefully we can cover our tracks," said Gruber.

They started to walk fast. Very soon they came to a riverbed. The moon was shining brightly in the sky. Its reflection illuminated the river water as if a thousand lamps were floating on it. The trees around them shone as if they were made of moonlight. For a monnet, the friends stopped and stared at the sight. It was breathtakingly beautiful and felt almost magical.

"I hear footsteps," said Glimp. He was correct. No sooner had he uttered those words than a group of five men approached them. Each man had a turban on his head. Their faces were covered with thick moustaches. They carried bags on their backs and had flame torches to guide them. None of them was talking. They were moving as if in a trance. *They must be on a mission of sorts,* thought Glimp. When the men saw Glimp, they stopped. The man ahead of the rest of the group looked at him suspiciously.

"What are you doing here?" he asked them, with his hand stretched out, ready to pull the spear out from behind him.

"Be careful of what you say. Don't mention anything about me," cautioned Gruber.

"I am lost in this mighty jungle. I just about lost hope before I saw you," Glimp blurted. The head of the group was not convinced.

"You must believe me. We were attacked by a mammoth. I narrowly escaped its wrath. Look at me," said Glimp. He was truly in disarray.

"You said 'we,' where is the other person?" enquired the chief.

"My friend was attacked by the mammoth. I could not see a thing in the darkness. I need help looking for him," said Glimp. He was not sure why he mentioned that, but he *was* feeling a bit guilty for having left Pompompulous in the cave to die. "We are disciples from the tutelage of Hermitus. We completed our studies and were on our way back home when this tragedy took place." Glimp was hoping the mention of his master's name might help. And it did.

As soon as he said that, the man addressed his group. "What are we waiting for? The master's disciples need our help. Let us look for the missing person." Each man pulled out his spear, ready to attack the mammoth as soon as they could see it.

"My name is Bugata. I am the head of the tribe that lives on the other side of the river. We were on our way from a hunt. Is there any other way we can help you?" he waited for Glimp to introduce himself.

"I'm Glimp, and I truly appreciate your help."

"I would be willing to give my life if it helped the master or any of his acquaintances," said Bugata. "Now where did the mammoth go from here?"

Glimp looked ahead. He could clearly see the three paths in front of them. But he could not recollect which path led to the cave. They had been lost for quite some time in the forest before they found the lepana.

"I think it's the path to the right," said Glimp. "I recognize it because I was dropping off twigs and rocks in heaps every now and then while we were walking."

"Good thinking on your part," said Bugata. Glimp felt uneasy; he was not used to being praised. Gruber looked annoyed. He did not want to go back to the cave. They all proceeded to walk in that direction.

As fate would have it, very soon they approached the cave where they had buried Pompompulous. The boulders at the cave entrance were thrown aside. Glimp almost fainted when he saw the entrance open. He staggered a little.

"What's the matter?" asked Bugata.

"This is where the mammoth attacked us. See the destruction around you, all the rocks thrown around and all the broken branches?" said Glimp. "This is where I lost my friend." He wanted to pretend he was crying, but his eyes filled up with actual tears. He truly felt sorry for Pompompulous.

Bugata cautioned everyone to stop. He went towards the cave, with his torch in one hand and his spear in the other. He looked inside. He twitched his nose as if he smelled something bad.

"There seems to be a dead and decaying body here," he said. Glimp's heart skipped a beat, as Bugata continued. "But I do not believe it to be your friend. It appears this body has been here for a while now. Here, come and give me a helping hand so that we can get closer to see what it is."

The men put their torches high up, so that the inside of the cave was filled with light. It was a bison. The bones were visible. The flesh appeared to have been eaten, for the most part. Whatever remained had decomposed. The stench was horrible.

The smell must have woken him up, thought Gruber. *But we now have witnesses to prove that we came back looking for him, just in case.*

As Bugata stepped outside the cave, his foot stepped on something that snapped under his weight. He picked it up. It was a bag.

"That must be mine. We lost our bags when we fought the monster," Glimp said as he took it from Bugata's hands.

"But there is still no sign of your friend," remarked Bugata.

"I'm not sure which way the mammoth went from here," said Glimp. He now knew that Pompompulous was alive, and he no longer wanted to find him.

At that point, one man from the tribe spoke. "No one has escaped the wrath of the mammoth before. You are lucky that the mammoth did not choose you. I suggest that we stop this search for now and come back during the day."

"I could not agree with you more," said Bugata. "Come with us and spend the night at the village. We will come back at dawn." Glimp, as suggested by Gruber, protested initially so that Bugata would not suspect their motives. Then they followed the tribe, hoping that they could rest peacefully at last. Soon they came to another riverbed. Bugata and his men crossed the still waters where it was shallowest. Glimp and Gruber followed them.

Chapter Thirteen
Karnika

Guard your faith, show mercy, pray and absolve.
Keep hope in despair, the grit to resolve.
Persist in difficult times, problems will solve.
Nights of darkness, into dawn they dissolve.

They were walking in another part of the forest when Andreux and Senfred heard footsteps behind them. They turned back and were surprised to see Glimp. There was no sign of Pompompulous.

"Where is Pompompulous?" Senfred asked him. Glimp gave out a sinister laugh.

"Dead is he, as dead can be," he replied and approached Senfred in a rather menacing way. Andreux drew his sword from its sheath. As soon as he did that, Glimp laughed wickedly and turned into a wild beast. Andreux quickly realized that it was some sort of black magic, and someone was playing cruel tricks with them. He attacked the beast. No sooner did he attack than the beast vanished into thin air. Senfred saw tiny sparks of light flying away. "Lumen-drobs!" he exclaimed. "This sure is a strange part of the forest."

"The master had warned us that something like this might happen. As long as we are prepared, there's nothing we need to fear," said Andreux. The friends remained vigilant as they continued their journey.

"I wonder where 'Pulous and Glimp are right now?" said Senfred. Then he suddenly stopped in his tracks as he saw a body disappear into the mist-filled darkness a little ahead of them. "I think I just saw Nevius."

"I'm not sure it wasn't another act of magic!" said Andreux. "We need to be on our guard."

"I don't think so. It was as if Nevius was fighting a gust of wind or something. He seemed to have fallen behind that bush over there. Let's look," Senfred insisted. But when they reached the bush, they found no one. On careful examination, they found some fresh footsteps on the ground.

"Let's not waste time looking for unseen enemies. I believe we're already behind our schedule. Let us pick up pace."

"Just give me a minute," said Senfred. He paused to listen. He was not sure if the sight of Nevius was another act of magic or if he had actually seen Nevius. He placed his ear on the ground to listen. He did not hear any footsteps. However, to his surprise, he heard two strange voices quarrelling. The voices he heard were of Fortuna and Ilvila.

"Why help them? The wind blows Nevius in their face, not on its own."

"Yet black magic they thought it was. Why attack them with beasts as their friends?"

Andreux looked at Senfred and asked him, "What are you doing?"

Senfred got up to tell Andreux what he just heard, but then he could no longer hear the conversation. He signalled Andreux to remain quiet and he put his ear back to the ground in the same spot. He heard the quarrelling voices again.

"Glimp-Gruber not their friend. Do I can what I want to. I answer not to you."

"Then warn them I will, no option I have."

"No good your help be 'cause have to deal with me, those wretched wanderers," said Ilvila.

"How dare you!" yelled Fortuna. "Nothing you are without me. Remember that!"

A fight seemed to follow the verbal duel. Senfred heard fisticuffs. He wondered where it was all happening. He could not see anyone, but he could hear every word. Just as he was about to lift his head, he heard a very different voice. It was authoritative.

"Fortuna and Ilvila!" the voice echoed in the forest. "You have caused enough trouble already. Your acts have interfered with the journey of these young men, which bears great significance to us all. I will not tolerate any more insolence on your part. Mend your ways or be prepared to face dire consequences."

After that there was silence. Senfred realized that it was all over for now. He raised his head from the ground. Senfred was surprised. Did he actually hear those voices or was it another unexplained act of magic? He looked at the spot where his head touched the ground. Was it the dim light from his glare crystal or did he see something shining in the grass? He ran his fingers across the wild grass that grew with abandon. He felt a little object that was hidden from human eyesight. He picked up the object and pointed his glare-crystal towards it.

It was an ear carved out of copper. There were intricate and exquisite carvings on it in a script that neither of them were familiar with. The ear had a metal clip that could hold it in place when it is was placed on one's own ear.

"Fantastic!" he said.

"What is it?" asked Andreux.

"It's a metal ear," said Senfred as he handed it to his friend. Andreux looked at it with keen interest. As Andreux observed it carefully, Senfred told Andreux what he had just heard. "And I could hear all that because of this ear, hidden in the grass. It seems to have the power of making inaudible voices audible to human ears," he added.

"If we found it here, it was not a coincidence. I'm sure we'll need it in the future," said Andreux as he put it on his ear.

"These human sojourners may need to relax, now that it is almost night," he heard an owl say.

"If they continue this way, they will pass by the ruined mansion," said its mate.

Andreux repeated what he heard to Senfred. "I name this ear *Karnika*," he said, and he gave the ear back to Senfred. Senfred carefully put it in his bag.

The friends continued walking and soon reached an old dilapidated mansion in the middle of the jungle. It was in ruins and covered with wild bushes and cobwebs. Andreux looked at the map and realized that this was where they had to halt for the night. There was no point in walking any further. But they had to make sure that the place was not inhabited before they could sleep there. Andreux and Senfred approached the ruins with caution. They cut through the cobwebs on the surrounding trees with their swords and looked inside. It was dirty, as if no one lived there. There was a little pond nearby, where they washed themselves. The cold water refreshed them and renewed them with new hope. In spite of a hectic day, full of adventures and unexpected twists and turns, the friends were not ready to sleep yet. They sat quietly, each lost in his own thoughts.

It was not by chance that the friends came across the shelter. Ilvila, in spite of warnings from forces of the forest, had decided to test them one last time. She waved her wands and filled up the place with dirt and dust, just as the friends stepped in to take a look at its interiors. She knew that the ogress would come very soon. If Senfred and Andreux could survive the ogress, it would be her final test.

Ogres and lumen-drobs, friends, foes and beasts.
The journey is full of adventures like these.
Just when you slow down and say "No more, please!"
along comes the next twist you expect the least.

"Hopefully we have not been delayed by the day's events," remarked Senfred.

"A little delayed, yes, but no need to panic yet. According to the map, we're another two megallids from the riverbed," said Andreux. "We can easily make up for the lost time." He looked around the dwelling one more time. There were cobwebs on the walls; a thick layer of dust settled on the floor.

"This place looks deserted," said Senfred.

"This is the dilapidated shelter that our master warned us about. We should continue to move along."

"But who would be living here now? Our master mentioned that it was used as a spy post a long time ago."

"I'm not sure. But we should be careful, nevertheless. After all the unnatural things that we've been experiencing today, I'm wary of anything that looks or smells suspicious," Andreux said. "Still, I agree with you. You said you heard voices with Karnika, indicating that the mischief was over for now."

"I did listen to someone chastising some others for their pranks on us earlier."

"Let's rest here for the night and have some food. We can take turns, so we won't be taken by surprise," Andreux suggested.

The friends removed their bags and took some food. As they ate, they reminisced about their childhood. "Remember the one time when you would not eat the puffed rice because you thought it was too hard!" Senfred said, laughing.

"And Mother said that there were scores of people who didn't have a full morsel of food for days."

"Aunt Arianne must have felt really bad then, knowing fully well that you, being a prince, had to live like that."

"What I miss the most is the fact that we had to live without knowing the truth behind our existence."

"Everything has changed so fast! I wonder what else awaits us in this quest?" said Senfred.

As he was about to reply, Andreux saw light descending from the sky and falling on the pillars behind them. There were different shades of light. Each ray fell on a different pillar. Andreux looked at the pillars. There were four pillars, each carved out of stone, and each had a different statue. The statues were those of celestials, who roamed freely in the skies. The sculpture was amazingly intricate, and the statues looked real. Just as Andreux looked at them, he saw a slight movement. He rubbed his eyes in disbelief. The statues were talking to one another. He could see their lips moving. Their heads turned to face one another, and their hands were moving as well. Andreux intuitively pulled Karnika from Senfred's bag and put it on his ear. As soon as he had it on, he could hear what the statues were talking about.

"Looks like we have company tonight," said the statue on the left corner.

"I wish they knew that this place belongs to an ogress. If they don't leave now, she will soon come and kill them," said the statue to its right.

"It is no better or worse than our fates, stuck here for the rest of eternity," groaned the statue on the right.

"It almost seems like the whole world is filled with stories of misfortune these days," said the statue on the left.

"Where have you been tonight, Venu?" asked the second statue from the right.

"I could not go far tonight Vanu. It feels like my powers are diminishing with each passing night." The other three nodded in agreement. Venu continued.

"I met a cuckoo that was in the city of Vauns," it said. These words heightened the curiosity of Andreux. He listened attentively.

"I heard the atrocities of Nefarius once again. The subjects of Vauns have suffered enough. It is time that the rightful heir took over the reins," said Venu.

"What happened tonight?" asked the statue next to it.

"The cuckoo told me that Nefarius has decided all people over four hogashes are a burden on his treasury. Consequently he has ordered them to leave his kingdom. Anyone found violating the rule will be executed as soon as they are caught. The rule came into effect yesterday, so there was a lot of scrambling in the city. I witnessed a lot of tearful good-byes. The young ones do not want the elders to leave. The elders do not want to endanger their lives or those of their beloved. Nefarius increased the patrol in the city so that he could capture all violators almost immediately."

"That is terrible. It almost feels like the reign of terror the Lord of Evil and Darkness unleashed on the Earth several hogashes ago," commented Vanu.

"It could very well be. I met a stag that was at the mines of Tragir tonight. Nefarius is in league with Morbidan. They have big plans to resurrect the Lord of Evil and Darkness. That is why they need manpower to work for them in the mines. Hence the order to banish men and women over four hogashes from the city—so that he gets free labour for his mines!" said the statue to its left.

"That is so cruel!" exclaimed Manu, another statue.

Andreux felt blood rushing into the veins in his temple. He felt furious listening to the statues. His subjects had suffered enough. He should have known long ago. He felt that his mother had protected him while the rest of Vauns had suffered, and he felt guilty.

"I met two serpents from Morgui Trail tonight. They were hissing that it is time for us to be free once again," said Vanu.

"Oh! How sweet those words taste!" exclaimed the three other statues.

"It feels like we have been stuck here forever." sighed Venu.

"The only way we can ever be truly free is when that demon dies," said Manu.

"And the only way she would die is when someone plucks the thorn from her head," said Vanu. "I hope that what I heard at Morgui Trail was true."

"Serpents at Morgui Trail do not lie," said the statue to his left. At that point, the statues became quiet.

Andreux could no longer contain his curiosity. He spoke to the statues.

"My name is Andreux and this is Senfred. We are on our way to Vauns and happened to stay here for the night. I do not wish to eavesdrop, but because of the magic ear, I was able to hear your conversation. I also apologise for interrupting, but if I may ask, why have you been held captive here and who caused this to you?"

The statues clearly became excited to hear him speak to them.

"He is talking to us." Exclaimed Vanu.

"Finally, after all these yedibs," said Venu.

"May be he is destined to kill the ogress and free us!" said Vanu.

"He is still waiting for our answers," commented Manu. Venu addressed Andreux.

"My name is Venu and these are my friends, Manu, Megu and Vanu. We are celestials who have been trapped in these statues by an ogress. Manu, do you remember that fateful day when we came looking for your wives?"

"How can I forget Venu? It was slightly over one and one-half hogashes ago. When Orna and Munora failed to show up for the celestial dance, we came here looking for them. The enchanted lake was their favourite hideout, but it was nowhere to be seen. Somehow we were trapped by the ogress," replied Vegu.

"And she has had us since then, trapped inside these pillars, unable to free ourselves from her spell."

"We can only wander for a few monnets every other lune, and that too not very far." Said Megu.

"Why can't you kill the ogress? Or contact other celestials to help free you?" asked Andreux.

"Our powers have all been usurped by the ogress. We are helpless." Confided Manu.

"But we can definitely help you. You see the ogress is very powerful, but all her powers are in her horn. If you can succeed in plucking her horn from her head, she will die and that will set us free." Said Venu.

"But you need to be quick. The ogress gets stronger by the moment." Cautioned Vanu.

When Andreux realized that the statues had stopped talking, he glanced at Senfred, who was looking at him enquiringly. Andreux repeated the conversation that he just heard.

"If what you just heard is true, then this place is not safe. We need to leave right away," said Senfred.

"I can't just leave knowing that innocent lives are trapped here. I have to get rid of the ogress and save the celestials," he said.

"But we can do that on our return from the city, can't we? We have an important task ahead of us."

"What will I tell our master, when I see him? That I failed to protect people that live within the borders of Vauntic Kingdom! What kind of an. explanation do I give to my mother or your father? That I'm not worthy of their hopes and aspirations? I know that we're on an important mission, but this is just as important," said Andreux.

Senfred became quiet for a monnet. They finished eating and packed their bags. Soon everything became quiet. The branches stopped swinging; the leaves did not rustle any more. The friends knew that the ogress was on her way. They both stood and waited at the entrance for her arrival.

The ogress did not keep them waiting. She was huge, to put it mildly. With locks of unkempt hair falling over her face, a sharp-pointed horn on her head, blood-red eyes and long canine teeth sticking out of her mouth, she was a terrible sight to behold. As soon as she landed in front of the shelter, she smelled the presence of human beings.

"Aha! I smell the blood of young humans. It has been a long time, hasn't it, since I had tasted human blood," she roared mightily. Andreux and Senfred stepped forward. The ogress stared at them. She was clearly angry.

"How dare you mess with what is not yours? Whose permission did you seek before you decided to step inside?" she yelled.

"This shelter is in Vauns and therefore rightfully belongs to us. Tell me your name and seek forgiveness," replied Andreux.

"Oho! A fearless human! You must taste wonderful! Come closer. Let me look at your baby face before I render it lifeless." She took a giant step towards them.

"Do not be fooled by appearances. Surrender to us and be spared."

She did not heed Andreux's advice. She came lunging towards them.

As soon as he saw the ogress approach them with her fists folded in, Senfred did not waste a single monnet. He pulled out his sword and attacked her. But even though he was quick, he was no match for the ogress. She muttered a spell under her breath and quickly increased her size. She grew to such a height that the shelter looked like her toy house. She then looked at Senfred, her eyes burning red with anger. She picked him up with her left thumb and index finger, gave him a look of contempt and then with a quick fling, threw him away. Before Andreux could realize what was happening, Senfred had fallen out of sight.

The ogress was not content with that. Her gaze now turned to Andreux. She lifted her foot and tried to crush him under it. Andreux ran back into the shelter and hid behind a pillar. The ogress could not see him. It took her a few monnets before she found him. The only way to kill him would be to destroy the shelter, but she did not want to demolish her dwelling. She started to shrink so that she could get inside. As soon as she started to shrink, one of the statues shouted to Andreux.

"Grab her horn! Grab her horn!"

When he heard that, Andreux recollected what the statues had been talking about earlier. The ogress's powers were all in the horn on her head. He had to pluck the horn in order to kill her. As soon as the ogress approached him, he went for her horn. He pulled at it with all his might. The ogress ran out of the shelter and started to increase in size again. Andreux held on to her horn. The ogress was gasping for life. She tried to catch him with both hands. As she grabbed him with one hand, Andreux slashed his sword and cut her right thumb. She let out a mighty roar. Just then Andreux jumped from her head to the top of her nose. As she looked at him, too stunned to realize what was happening, he pierced both her eyes with his sword.

"Take that, you monster!" he shouted angrily. "That's for all the innocent lives that you held captive in this shelter." The ogress, now blinded, tried to shake him off her face with a violent nodding of her head. But Andreux was quicker than she expected. He jumped back on her head as she rapidly started to decrease in size. She had almost dropped to the size of an elf when he cut off her horn with his sword in one smooth strike.

The ogress gave out a loud cry. She fell to the ground with her hands clutching her heart, as blood poured out of her eyes, nose and mouth. Her hands and legs shook as she regained her normal size.

Andreux watched the ogress as she died. He had never killed anyone before. He had never expected to in his lifetime. But here he was. He felt very uneasy. The anger that had taken control over his senses now subsided. He looked at his sword that was stained with the ogress's blood. He had no right to kill anyone, but then had he had a choice? Maybe he did.

He did not have time to ponder it now. He heard a rumbling sound. He looked at the shelter, and to his astonishment, the celestials that were trapped in it as statues were regaining their true forms. Just as they left the pillars and stepped outside, the shelter exploded. Andreux ran as far away as possible. He waited for the noise to subside. The stone pillars and the roof made of rocks splintered into fragments, big and small, which flew everywhere. The shelter was now reduced to a heap of broken rocks and stone, and the body of the ogress was buried underneath the debris.

The celestials approached Andreux. They folded their hands and bowed their heads to him. They were all taller than Andreux. Their feet floated in the air. They wore robes of silk that shone like gold. Their robes were adorned with rare and precious jewels and had white-feathered wings on their shoulders. One of them stepped forward and addressed him. "We are forever indebted to you for saving us from spending an eternity in that shelter, O fearless one.

We wish you all the best in your endeavour. Travel to your right and you will find your friend, well and alive. Then climb the tallest tree that you can see. You will find the way to Vauns."

With that the celestials flapped their wings and rose from the forest. They waved at Andreux as they flew out of sight.

Andreux watched the celestials fly away. With Karnika still on his ear, he went in search of Senfred. Maybe he should have listened to him and left the ogress alone. What would happen if Senfred had been killed or badly injured? Could he ever forgive himself if such a thing had happened tonight? He was comforted by the fact that his friend was still alive. He had to find him. They had to get to Vauns. He was not sure how much time was lost, but he decided to forego sleep for the rest of the night.

Where could Senfred have fallen? thought Andreux as he searched for him in the direction shown by the celestials. He could not find him anywhere. As Andreux kept looking for any signs that would lead him to Senfred, he saw muddy footprints and broken branches farther away. His heart pounded as he raced to that spot. He looked around, but he did not find anyone there. There were a lot of signs indicating that there was a struggle some time ago, but there was no body.

He continued to follow the footprints cautiously. However, he lost track of the footprints after a few monnets. They seemed to end abruptly near the base of a Capirona bark, which seemed to reach out to the skies. Andreux climbed up the tree with difficulty as the outer bark peeled off as soon as he placed his hands on it. When he climbed up, he saw a very tall tree not very far from where he stood. *That must be the tallest tree in this part of the forest,* he said to himself. *That must be the tree that the celestials suggested that I climb.* Then he saw something unexpected.

Pompompulous was attending to Senfred, who was unconscious on the ground. Pompompulous looked as if he had come straight from war. He was limping, using a broken branch as a makeshift crutch.

What happened to Pompompulous? Where is Glimp? Andreux was surprised by the sudden turn of events. Then he saw Glimp hiding behind a tree. *Why is he hiding behind the tree?* he wondered.

Determined to find out, Andreux jumped down. But unfortunately, he fell into a pit covered by leaves and twigs. As he fell, he hit his head against a rock protruding from the side and everything went black.

Make amends while you can; you live but once.
The guilt that you carry, if not, is immense.
Words and arguments you build in your defence
may convince others; your soul seeks penitence.

"Eat to your heart's content," Bugata offered, but Glimp could hardly eat a morsel.

A lantern was burning in the corner, but otherwise it was pitch dark in the hut where Glimp and Gruber were resting. They had followed Bugata and his tribesmen to their village. The path had been long and winding, yet the fact that they were in the company of men who knew the surroundings had made the walk easier. They had remained quiet for the most part, and once they reached the village, Glimp quickly cleaned himself.

Soon Glimp was fed and shown a bed. Glimp, still trying to come to terms with everything that had happened, was too numb to appreciate the hospitality that was being showered upon him.

"You should sleep now. The journey has worn you out," Bugata advised before he left the hut.

After he left, Glimp waited a few monnets before he cleared his throat. "What do we do now, Gruber? I feel like we can't stay here any longer." He was hopeful—if not certain—that Gruber would know the way out of this mess. However, Gruber was very quiet.

"Do you know what would happen if Bugata came to know the truth?" Gruber said, and he lifted his right index finger and slid it across his throat.

"Then let's get out of here, right now," suggested Glimp.

"But how? Will they not suspect us if we disappear without their knowledge?" Gruber did not want to forego the hospitality. Glimp, however, was beginning to suspect that all doors had closed on them at once.

"I think I have an answer for that," he said as he pulled out a piece of papyrus from his robe and scribbled a few illegible words on it. He then showed it to Gruber. The papyrus was old and crumpled in the corners. The letters were scrawny and went up and down as if they were riding a wave.

We must find our friend.
Cannot stay.
Thanks for everything.

"Are you sure about this?" asked Gruber.

"Never felt more certain of anything before," replied Glimp.

"I must caution you then, you will be on your own. I cannot come with you."

"Then so be it," said Glimp, as he felt his heart getting lighter, as if a heavy weight was being lifted off his chest. "I am going now. I think I've already overstayed my welcome here."

Glimp and Gruber got up without making any noise. Glimp stuck the papyrus to the doorknob. It was dark outside. There were no lights to be seen in any of the nearby huts. After they made sure that no one was watching them, they quickly slipped into the darkness. They walked gingerly in the shade until they reached the river. They crossed the river at its shallow end, just as Bugata showed them earlier. The river water was cold and calm. The friends climbed the bark of a huge tree that fell across the river.

"This is where we part ways," said Gruber. "From here you will be on your own." He disappeared as Glimp crossed the river. When he approached the forest, Glimp was wet and shivering. He dried himself and applied lepana on his eyes.

"Let us go and find our friend Pompompulous," said Glimp. He realized immediately that he was alone now. Gruber was no longer with him, and Glimp almost missed him. He thought he heard a faint voice nearby. "Are you missing me, Glimp?"

"No. I am not," he told himself. As he started walking towards the cave, he heard an explosion. The ground on which he stood shook a little and the trees swayed back and forth dangerously.

"What was that?" exclaimed Glimp. He was frightened out of his wits. As he looked around, he thought he saw something move behind a nearby bush. He tiptoed carefully towards the bush. After a few steps, he could see a body slumped on the ground. However, it was not Pompompulous, as he had suspected. It was Senfred.

Instinctively, he walked towards Senfred to help him, but as he approached him, he heard the voice of Pompompulous.

"Oh! What happened to you, Senfred? Did Glimp get you too? Where is Andreux?"

Glimp jumped behind a tree just as Pompompulous appeared. Pompompulous was bruised and his clothes showed signs of struggle. His face was puffed, cheeks were swollen and one eye was black. He had his bag on his back and carried a glare crystal in his left hand. His right hand held a thick broken branch that he used to support himself as he limped with difficulty towards Senfred.

Chapter Sixteen
Vicious Circle

In moments of despair, when man plays divine
a trishank is figmented, real and sublime,
to hold on to something that got lost in time,
to keep happy memories fresh and alive.

"*Vilep*[12] should help wake him up," Pompompulous said to himself. He sprinkled some water on Senfred's face and put some smelling salts near his nose. Senfred slowly opened his eyes.

When he saw Pompompulous, he was dazed for a monnet. "Where am I? Where's Andreux? How did you find me?"

"We're both in the jungle. And I wanted to ask you the same thing. What happened to you?"

Senfred explained to Pompompulous about their short stay at the dilapidated shelter and Andreux's fight with the ogress.

"Then we must find Andreux at once. He might need our help," said Pompompulous, helping Senfred up from the ground.

Senfred held his head tightly. He still had his sword in his hand. He put it back in its sheath. Then he took a long look at Pompompulous. "Whatever happened to you? Where is Glimp?"

"I can explain that in greater detail later. But for now, it's sufficient to say that Glimp tried to kill me and shoved me in a cave, leaving me for dead. He is with Nevius, has been all along. He has an alter ego, calls himself Gruger or Gruber, who is very unlike Glimp, cunning and ruthless. I somehow managed to survive," he said.

"I wish I had seen through his plans. I'm sorry that you had to be subjected to all that, my friend," said Senfred as he picked up his bag. Glimp, who was still hiding behind the tree, came rushing forward and fell on their feet. He was trembling with fear.

---

12   The word *vilep* is a term for "smelling salts."

As soon as he saw Glimp, Senfred pulled out his sword once again. "What audacity you display, coming to us again. You deserve to die after what you have done to 'Pulous," he shouted angrily.

Glimp cried out in fear. His lips were trying to utter something, but it was not at all audible. He managed to stammer out a few words. "Please forgive me. It wasn't my fault. I never wanted to harm anyone. I shouldn't have listened to Gruber. The lumen-drobs tricked me as well."

Pompompulous looked in Glimp's eyes. The unspoken fear was real, but he could not tell if the spoken words were true as well. "Get away from here as soon as you can, before Senfred actually kills you," he warned him.

"But I was telling the truth," protested Glimp.

"If what you said was the truth, then we are better off without you. Heed the words of Pompompulous and leave immediately. A few more monnets, and I may give in to the temptation of revenge. Now run for your life," Senfred said.

Glimp stood up, picked up his bags, saying, "I am sorry for what I've done to you. I'll certainly make amends in this lifetime. I hope to be of use to you soon." And with that, he ran out of sight.

Pompompulous watched as Glimp slipped out of sight. *I hope that is the last time that we meet him,* he thought.

As they started to walk back towards the shelter, Senfred asked Pompompulous if he wanted to join him in looking for Andreux.

"Of course I will. After what just happened, I think I'll be better off with you. Moreover, I think we're closer to the city now, so I could actually be of use to you," he said.

"As I fell, I heard an explosion from behind," said Senfred. "It must have been the shelter."

"I hope Andreux is unharmed," Pompompulous replied.

Looking for Andreux, they wandered farther away from where he had fallen. The pit in which Andreux remained unconscious was hidden from sight. They walked to the shelter and found it broken apart. They found the body of the ogress under the rubble, but there was no sign of Andreux anywhere.

"It looks like Andreux killed the ogress. I wonder what caused the shelter to explode?" Senfred commented.

"Then where's Andreux? And what about the statues that you both saw?" asked Pompompulous. They both looked through the debris but could not find any statues.

"The celestials must have been freed with the death of the ogress."

"That still leaves us with the question of Andreux's whereabouts," said Pompompulous.

"He must have gone looking for me," said Senfred.

"Let's wait here for some time then. He might return to this spot once again," said Pompompulous. Just then Senfred walked past a dense bush, and to the utter astonishment of Pompompulous, he disappeared into thin air as he stepped forward. Pompompulous waited for a monnet or two and then with a slight hesitation, he followed Senfred. When he looked at himself, he could see his body clearly. *But have I disappeared too?* he wondered. He found Senfred walking a little ahead of him. He still seemed to be looking for whatever he found moving behind the bushes.

"Senfred! Wait for me," shouted Pompompulous. Senfred looked back, and Pompompulous could see the bewilderment in his eyes. Instinctively, he followed Senfred's gaze.

The debris that they'd left behind was no longer visible. In its place was a beautiful garden, full of colourful flowers and fruits. There were multitudes of birds perched in the branches of trees and singing sweetly.

"We've walked into a magic land, it appears," said Senfred.

"Let's try to get back to the debris. We need to find Andreux," said Pompompulous. The friends retraced their steps, but to no avail.

"What do we do now?" asked Pompompulous.

"We have to keep looking for the way back, I guess," said Senfred.

There was no sign of debris. There was no sign of a forest either. The beautiful garden seemed to surround them in whichever direction they went. It spread across the land as far as they could see.

"This sure beats any logic," said Senfred.

"I think I've had enough magic for this lifetime," complained Pompompulous. As they walked a little further, the two friends saw a small pond filled with bright red lotus flowers floating on the water. Instinctively, Senfred put out his hand to grab a flower and the flower grabbed him instead. He was pulled into the pond, and he disappeared out of Pompompulous's sight once more.

"Oh boy," said Pompompulous, and he followed his friend into the pond. He felt himself falling through a vast mass of water. He could barely keep his eyes open as he fell. He was rapidly being pulled towards the bottom of the pond. He could not believe that such a little pond could have so much water in it. As his feet touched the bottom of the pond, he steadied himself and looked around. To his surprise, there was no water. He looked up. There was water high above, as if it were the sky.

"This is all so weird," he mumbled as he looked for Senfred. He found him nearby.

"I don't know what came over me! I felt as if someone was pulling me towards the flower," said Senfred.

"Must be strong magic, to influence someone like that," said Pompompulous.

Senfred scratched his head. "We must find our way out of this."

"As long as you don't take us anywhere else from here."

"But where are we now? And how do we get out of this place?" asked Senfred. They walked ahead to find out. A little later, they came across an old man. He was barely able to walk. He was thin, his bones showing through his skin. He was walking with a limp and carrying a big basket of fruit on his head. The basket looked as if it would fall any monnet. His eyes had an empty look, like that of a glass crystal.

"Could you please tell us where we are?" asked Senfred.

"And could you also tell us the way to Vauntic Kingdom from here?" asked Pompompulous.

The man looked at them. The friends felt as if he looked through them. He continued to walk as if he did not hear them.

"Let me help you with your burden," said Senfred as he tried to lift the basket. The old man suddenly jumped up and down as if life had returned to him.

"Thieves! Looters! Robbers! Mercenaries! Get away from me and my basket or I will kill you!" he shouted angrily.

Senfred and Pompompulous stepped back. They were taken aback by the old man's angry utterances.

"Let us leave him and move on," suggested Pompompulous.

And so they walked past the old man. After a few more steps, they met two little boys who were playing in front of a small house. They were playing catch with a ball. They seemed to be preoccupied with their game; when Senfred called them, they did not respond.

"Did you look at them?" asked Senfred.

"They sure looked odd to me," replied Pompompulous.

"They have very mature faces for boys," said Senfred.

They continued to walk.

Soon they came across a woman attending to her child. The mother was blissfully unaware of what was happening around her. She seemed to enjoy every moment with her daughter. The little girl had bright twinkling eyes, but again she had very mature features as well. It almost looked as if the baby girl had her mother's face.

"Excuse me," said Senfred as he addressed the woman. She did not bother to look at the strangers.

"Look at that!" exclaimed Pompompulous as he noticed a gigantic snake slither in the background. He grabbed his sword, his legs shaking with fear. But he had no cause to be afraid. The snake disappeared as quickly as it appeared.

"This sure is a funny place," said Senfred as they continued walking. They walked for a long time before they met anyone else.

They next met a young man who was frantically looking for something he had apparently lost. Again, this man, though he had the physique of a youth, had an aging face.

"Excuse me, sir," Pompompulous cleared his throat as he addressed the man. The man stopped looking around. He lifted his face and looked at them questioningly. "Yes?"

"Finally, someone noticed us," said Senfred, with relief. "We're lost in this place and were wondering if you knew the way to Vauns?" The man laughed bitterly when he heard this. "If I knew my way out, would I still be here? I've been looking for the way out myself," he said.

"People must be trapped here under some sort of enchantment," Pompompulous observed. He had a rising fear. "How long have you been lost here, sir?" he asked the man, who had resumed his search for the way out.

"I'm not sure. It almost feels like I've been here all my life. Let me think. I was on my way to meet my general." He paused. He became cautious at once. "Now wait a minute. Why are you asking me all these questions? Who are you? Are you Vauntic spies?"

"No we're not. We're lost in this place, just like you are," said Senfred assuring the man. This seemed to calm him. The frown disappeared from his face.

"Well then, there is no harm in talking to you. Hopefully you'll get me out of this place as well. Yesterday, or rather, the day before I accidentally walked into this maze, the Vauntic Kingdom was celebrating the news of Queen Minerva's pregnancy. So that's how long I've lost touch with the outside world. So tell me, who is the king now?" he asked.

"Nefarius," replied Pompompulous. Did he see a smile flicker on the man's lips?

"One and one-half hogashes!" exclaimed Senfred.

"What did you say?" asked the man.

"That's how long you've been lost in this maze," said Senfred. "What kind of a place is this?" The smile disappeared from the man's face. Senfred and Pompompulous looked dejected as well. They did not want to spend one and one-half hogashes in this place. "Whatever it is, we'll find our way out. Now let's move on," said Pompompulous. The man stayed back, still trying to find his way out.

"He must've gone mad after all these yedibs!" said Senfred.

"I think I know who the man is," said Pompompulous.

"What! How do you know him? Why didn't you tell him then?" asked Senfred.

"I don't know him well enough to talk to him, but I know of him," said Pompompulous.

"Who is he?"

"Do you remember the night before we started off on this journey, when I told you about what happened when Andreux was about to be born? A spy was sent to inform Nefarius, but somehow was never able to reach him. I strongly suspect this man is that spy."

"Yes. That does seem to add up," said Senfred. He became quiet. Then all of a sudden, he exclaimed, "I think we are lost in a vicious circle; that's what it is!"

"You mean a *trishank*[13]?" asked Pompompulous.

"In thinking about it, I'm certain that's where we're stuck now."

"How do we get out of it?" asked Pompompulous.

"From what our master taught us, we need to find the pattern of events in the trishank. That will reveal the patch that joins the beginning and end of the vicious circle into an infinite loop. And in order to find that, we need to keep walking until we start to see things and people repeating themselves."

"What if the trishank is too long? How do we get to the end? And when we see the end, how do we know that it is in fact the end?" Pompompulous felt drained.

"Don't lose heart yet, 'Pulous. Andreux must be waiting for us. We need to get out of this and help him. Now let's keep walking. And look out for any odd patterns," said Senfred.

While they walked, the first object that caught Pompompulous's eye was a lumen-drob following them. He remembered what Glimp had told him, just before they got trapped in the trishank. *The lumen-drobs tricked us once. Could they be tricking us again?* he thought.

They kept walking. They walked past two men sitting under the shade of a birch tree and talking. The friends stopped to listen to their conversation.

"I hope that the harvest season will be good this yedib. It has been three yedibs since we had a good crop."

"If not, then I have no choice but to sell my farm and join the king's army."

"But the king has declared war on the neighbouring kingdom. What if you get enrolled in the war?"

"I am not sure I have any choice."

---

13   A *trishank* is a "vicious circle" or "time loop" created by someone to suit his or her own needs or desires, in which time is frozen over a limited period.

"What will your family do when you go away? How will they survive?"

"The king promised to take care of them, didn't he?"

"The king will say whatever it takes to enlist men in his army."

"But then ...?"

"Listen to me. Do not give up hope yet. Wait for the harvest season before you decide anything."

"We have not had a good crop for three yedibs. It did not rain at all this yedib. Downpour is almost over, but not a single drop of rain yet!"

"The king's prophet predicted heavy rain the next few days, didn't he?"

"I hope that will keep us from starving this yedib."

"You really don't want to enlist in the army then, do you?"

"Not if I had a choice."

"But you do have a choice."

"What about hope? It is not enough to have a choice when there is no hope."

"All is not lost yet. The god will take care of us poor farmers. We will have a good harvest this yedib."

"What makes you so sure about it?"

"I am not sure. I just hope that the harvest season will be good this yedib. It has been three yedibs since we had a good crop."

"If not, then I have no choice but to sell my farm and join the king's army."

"But the king has declared war on the neighbouring kingdom. What if you get enrolled in the war?"

Senfred and Pompompulous quickly realized that the conversation itself was a loop. But try as they might, they could not find the beginning or ending in the conversation.

"It means this is not the event that has caused the trishank," remarked Senfred.

The friends continued walking. Soon they lost track of time and distance. Without realizing it, they walked for about three days and nights. They met fighting elephants, singing parrots, playing children and blooming flowers. None of them had any odd patch in their loops. Pompompulous became disheartened. "We'll never be able to get out of this place," he said. Suddenly he came upon the old man they had met first.

"Now wait a minute. We've completed the entire circle once. We've seen it all. We now have to figure out where the odd patch is," exclaimed Senfred.

Hope returned to Pompompulous once again. This time they did not bother talking to the old man. The old man did not seem to recognize them. Pompompulous remembered the lumen-drob that had been following them. He turned around to look for it. He could still see it. *Could the lumen-drob have tricked them?* His suspicion grew stronger. Maybe the lumen-drob would show them the time patch! As they continued, Pompompulous kept looking back to see if the lumen-drob still followed them. Soon they passed the two playing boys. They observed them for some time but again could not find any time patch.

Then they walked past the woman playing with her child. The lumen-drob still followed them. The giant snake appeared again and within a few monnets disappeared. Just as the snake disappeared, the lumen-drob seemed to shine a little bit.

"That's odd," said Pompompulous.

"What?" asked Senfred.

Pompompulous told him what he saw.

"Then let's walk back to see what happens," said Senfred. And they both took a few steps back. To their amazement, the events seemed to go back with each step. They soon went back to the old man. They started to walk ahead again, slowly and cautiously this time, noticing every slight change that they could see.

They came back to the woman playing with her child. Pompompulous noticed that just as the snake appeared, the lumen-drob disappeared. It reappeared as soon the snake disappeared. The lumen-drob must have assumed the form of the snake! "I found it! The time patch! I found the time patch!" exclaimed Pompompulous.

They approached the woman playing with her child. For a brief monnet, just before the snake disappeared, they could see a slight stir in her eyes. The image of the snake reflected in her pupils for a fleeting monnet. Her eyes quivered with fear and uncertainty. But all of a sudden, the image of the snake disappeared and the lumen-drob appeared a split second later. The uncertainty in her eyes was instantaneously replaced with joy and happiness.

"I think that the snake attempted to kill the child. The mother must've created this trishank to create her own world, free from death," guessed Senfred.

They approached her cautiously, knowing that she held great magical powers. Senfred cleared his throat to get her attention. The mother continued to ignore them as she played with her child.

"Excuse me, do you know how to remove the spell and get us out of this trishank?" he asked her.

The woman, who was oblivious to their presence before, stopped for a second when she heard him mention the spell. She turned her gaze towards them.

"You are very clever. But I have great joy in reliving these few moments that I had with my daughter. Why would I want to remove the spell and lose it all?"

"What actually happened? Whom did the snake kill; was it you or your child?" asked Senfred.

Tears gleamed in her eyes. "My daughter, of course," she said. "If I had not cast the trishank, then my daughter would have died from the snake venom. And so I cheated death."

"We are on our way to an important task. We got pulled into the vicious circle through no fault of ours. We request you to show us the way out," pleaded Pompompulous.

The woman laughed when she heard this. "Don't you know that there is no way out!"

The finality in her voice scared Pompompulous. But Senfred persisted. "You have to get us out. Otherwise, we'll create a counter-trishank for you right here," he said. He saw a stir in her eyes again, similar to when she first saw the snake approach her child.

"You cannot do that," she said.

But Pompompulous could tell she was not confident that her words were true.

"Then we will see," said Senfred as he pulled out his wand. The woman wavered as soon as she saw the wand.

"No wait. We need to talk," she pleaded with them. She looked at them both, trying to gauge her own difficult position. "If I do remove the time patch, can I ask you for a favour?"

"It depends on what type of favour that you would ask," said Senfred.

"I have spent quite some time with my daughter. In fact, longer than if she had lived. Will you promise to kill the snake before she bites my daughter?" she asked.

"But even if we kill the snake, your daughter will still die as soon as the trishank is broken, will she not? Her age will catch up with her." asked Senfred.

"That is quite true. But as a mother, I would rather she die a natural death than suffer a snake bite. Now, will you both promise me that you'll kill the snake before it bites my daughter?" she asked once again.

"We will," Senfred assured her.

The woman looked at her daughter for one last time. There was immense pleasure in her eyes, but it mingled with the pain of impending separation. Then she closed her eyes, parted her lips and quietly chanted a spell.

Suddenly the gigantic serpent emerged from the background and leapt towards the little child in the woman's arms. Senfred quickly slashed it into two pieces with his sword. The snake fell to the ground, decapitated.

No sooner than the snake died, the woman and her daughter started to age rapidly. As the friends watched, the baby in the mother's arms grew up to be a little girl, then a young woman, an old lady and shrivelled all in a matter of a few monnets. Soon mother and daughter both turned to ashes; two lives lost in front of the friends' eyes.

"The spell is removed," said Pompompulous as they both started to float upwards through the pond and then out of the garden and into the forest once again.

They both looked around. They were back where they had entered the trishank, near the debris of the ruined shelter.

"You did it, my friend," said Pompompulous excitedly.

"Now let us find Andreux," said Senfred.

As they walked by, they saw a skeleton lying in the nearby thorn bushes. Pompompulous recognized the chain around its neck. "The spy that we met in the vicious circle!" he exclaimed. "He lost his life without ever knowing the outcome."

They had barely taken a few steps when there was a commotion behind them. A group of men hiding behind bushes, their faces smeared with black and red paint jumped out and surrounded the two friends. They held sharp daggers in their hands. One of them, apparently their leader, was dressed in dark brown robe. He addressed them in a stern voice. "What do you have in your bags?"

Senfred pulled out his sword from its sheath. "In the name of Queen Minerva, I order you to lay down your weapons and surrender."

Pompompulous was terrified, and his legs trembled violently. He hung his head in fear, and his gaze never left the ground below his feet.

Before Senfred could attack the intruders, one of the bandits yelled, "Stop! We mean no harm to you. If you speak of our queen, then we are your allies."

Senfred stiffened as the bandit leader came closer. "I don't believe you. You're no more than a bunch of bandits. This must be one of your tricks," said Senfred, unmoved by the leader's assurance. But the bandit leader did not give up. "In the name of my King Reganor and Queen Minerva, I, Prosperus, mean no harm to you. To prove my word, I am hereby laying down my dagger."

As soon as they heard his name, the friends looked at the bandit leader and then at one another. A smile spread on the face of Pompompulous. "Father! Its me, your 'Pulous!" The leader paused and looked at Pompompulous, whose face was now red with emotion.

"This must be my lucky day!" he shouted joyfully, and he threw his arms around Pompompulous, drawing him into a tight hug. "'Pulous, my son! It's been such a long time since I've seen you!" Pompompulous looked up to see his father for the first time since he had been forced to live in exile. Tears rolled down their cheeks as they remained locked in an embrace.

Senfred was overcome with emotion as well. "What an unexpected turn of events!" he said. "I've heard so much about you from your son. It's an honour to meet you."

"Father, I'd like you to meet my friend Senfred, son of the minister-in-exile, Veritus," Pompompulous said as he wiped his tears.

"Why! I am ... This is unbelievable. It only seems to be getting better. So the rumour is true then, isn't it?" Prosperus's voice shook with excitement.

"Yes it is. The queen and her son, the prince, are very much alive," said Pompompulous.

"Andreux was with us just a little while ago, when we parted ways and got caught in a vicious circle. We must find him before Nevius or Glimp can cause him any harm," reminded Senfred.

"Then let's start right now," said Prosperus, "We can always catch up later." They started looking for Andreux. However, Senfred and Pompompulous did not know that they were very far from where Andreux was, in another part of Aranya.

In an old ruined temple, evil resides,
lost to the humans, but it did survive.
Now is the time for the past to revive;
the statue of Levitor can come back alive.

Andreux regained consciousness the next day, and for a monnet he was not sure where he was. Then he remembered seeing his friends before he fell into the trap. He tried to climb out of the pit, but there was nothing to hold on to. The soil was slippery and there were no roots or rocks protruding into the pit. After a few futile attempts, Andreux shouted for help. "Senfred! Pompompulous! Help me. I'm stuck in this pit behind you, under the giant Capirona!" But there was no response to his cries for help. As he struggled to get up, he realized that his bag fell with him. He opened it and searched its contents. He pulled two small knives out of his bag, put the bag on his back and started to climb up the pit, using them to dig into the soil and make steps. When he was halfway through the climbing, rays of light fell into the pit. Andreux was blinded by the light, but he looked up to see where it was coming from. He saw what appeared to be two fairies, one dressed in green, and the other in blue.

"Can you please help me get out of this pit?" he asked them.

"We sure can, O handsome prince!" said Fortuna.

"Who are you? How do you know that I am a prince?" he asked, looking at them suspiciously.

The lumen-drobs laughed when they heard his questions. "A lot more about you we know than imagine you can. Following you we have been, for some time now," confessed Ilvila.

"You must be the lumen-drobs then," said Andreux. "Then you can surely help me find my friends."

"Only help you we will, if help us you will in return," bargained Fortuna.

"What is it that I can do for you?" asked Andreux as he continued climbing. Ilvila waved her wand and his knives became stuck in the soil. However hard Andreux tried, he could not pull them out. He looked at the lumen-drobs with anger and frustration. "What is it that you both want?" he asked.

"Now, now. No need for impatience, is there? Too much fun we had with your group. So it happens that from Aranya banished we might be because of that. See our plight, do you?" asked Fortuna.

"No I don't. And frankly they should've stripped you both of your powers rather than let you loose on the world," said Andreux.

"Well, well! Ignorance, you are filled with, O mortal. Beyond Aranya, we are powerless, don't you see!" Ilvila said.

"You're testing my patience and wasting my time. What is it that you need?"

"In getting out of this pit, help you we will, and also in finding your friends," said Fortuna.

"You we will help in getting your kingdom back as well," continued Ilvila.

"If only you will ..." Fortuna paused melodramatically.

"... each day, send us one human being ..." added Ilvila.

"... our magic and mischief, who will satisfy," Fortuna finished.

Andreux's face reddened when he heard this. "Not in this life. I don't need your help at all. Now if you may kindly get out of my way, I have work to do," he said as he pulled the knives with all his might.

"So shall it be then," said the lumen-drobs in unison as they laughed wickedly and disappeared in a flash of light. To his utter dismay, Andreux found himself at the bottom of the pit once more. His knives had disappeared.

But he was not the type of person to lose hope so soon. Andreux looked around again to see if he could find anything to help him climb out of the pit. As before, he did not find anything at all. Then he searched for the holes dug by the knives earlier. He used these holes for support as he climbed up with his hands, but it was not an easy climb.

He repeatedly fell back to the bottom. Still, that did not deter him. He tried a few more times.

After three unsuccessful attempts, he managed to climb halfway up. His hands ached as his fingers bore his entire body weight. His hands bled and a few nails were chipped; his knees were scraped. After he reached the halfway point, Andreux could see a dim light falling into the pit. He wondered if it was daytime already. He continued to climb, with increasing hope and determination. As he dug holes with his bare hands to go up further, his entire body ached. Very soon he managed to climb out of the pit.

Once he was out of the pit, he climbed a nearby tree and looked for his friends. However, he did not find any of them. It was not sunrise yet. The light that had fallen into the pit was coming from nearby. Quickly he climbed down the tree and walked towards the light. As he walked towards the light, for a moment Andreux thought he saw Senfred and Pompompulous. They were walking away from him, obviously lost in their conversation. But they did not see him. Just as Andreux was about to call them, they disappeared out of his sight. He went in their direction, but could not find them.

"I hope that I'll meet them soon," he thought as he retraced his steps. As he continued walking, he saw an old ruined temple. He remembered what had happened with the ogress; however, he chose to ignore his master's caution. This was the third destination, the most dangerous one. Andreux decided to look into the temple to see if he could find any help in locating his friends.

As he walked towards the temple, he heard a faint voice. It was too faint to recognize whether it was a man or a woman. The voice, however, cast a spell on him immediately. Andreux went into the temple in a trance.

The temple was filled with dust and lack of care over several yedibs, maybe hogashes. In the centre of the temple was a huge statue covered with cobwebs and vines. The statue stood on a pedestal, which was cracked on all sides, due to the efflux of time. Yet the pedestal held a polished mirror that was shining like new. The mirror had words engraved on it in gold. The same words flashed on the mirror every now and then. Andreux paused to read them.

Hail the Mighty Lord; Hail Levitor!
Hail the Great Master, the one for us all.
He who was banished will soon come to life
to rule us, protect us and save us from strife.

As he read, new words replaced the old ones on the mirror.

If to me, myself, your life you can give,
I promise you, cross my heart, you will receive
more than what your mind can likely conceive:
life, fame and fortune, if only you believe.

It sounded too good to be true. What if one killed himself in the hope of getting everything and never came back to life? *Only fools would do such a thing!* Andreux thought. As the thought crossed his mind, he felt a sharp pain shooting up his chest, but it passed quickly. Out of curiosity, he removed the cobwebs and vines that had spread all over the statue to see it more clearly. He was taken aback when he saw Levitor's monstrous figure. The sight was revolting and terrified Andreux for a brief monnet. He gasped and stepped back involuntarily. As he did so, he sensed movement behind him and turned swiftly to see if there was anyone other than himself in the temple.

He found no one. There was, however, a water cascade flowing down the wall. What he perceived to be someone else had been his own reflection in the water. *There is something different about my image,* thought Andreux as he saw his reflection. The rock wall was uneven and covered with moss, and as a result, his image was not very clear. When Andreux took a closer look, he realized what was different about his reflection.

Though it was his face, it was not himself that he was looking at. The image had royal garments and a crown filled with jewels. The man in the image was strikingly handsome with thick, bushy eyebrows, a strong nose, high cheekbones, a square jaw and strong, muscular shoulders. His robes were decked with pearls and jewels.

Andreux was surprised to see himself as someone else. As he looked, the image disappeared and words appeared randomly across the cascade.

Welcome to Artheur. We meet once again.

Is this a mistake or a trick? Andreux wondered where he heard that name before. At that moment, he remembered his master's caution. *This place may be more dangerous than it appears.* He decided to move along. Just as he was about to leave the temple, he heard a feeble cough. Andreux turned back and looked inside. He found an old man lying in one corner. The man was very old, with white, long flowing beard that seemed to have grown to his knees. He wore shrivelled robes that hung loosely on his thin frame. Numerous wrinkle lines crossed his forehead.

"Who are you sir? What are you doing here?" asked Andreux.

The old man spoke in a whisper. "Come closer. I am a little hard of hearing."

Andreux went closer to him. The man must not have had a bath for a long time. The stench was unmistakable. Andreux asked him again. "Who are you sir? And what keeps you here?"

"I am an old magician, my child. The cascade you saw was my creation," he said.

"But why are you still here? Who looks after you?"

"I have no one in this world. As I said, I am a magician. But I have lost all interest in material gains. So here I am, living the life of a recluse."

"But why here, of all the places?" asked Andreux.

"Good question. It is not by pure chance that you find me here. I have spent my life trying to locate this temple. The statue that you see here, behind you, is that of a man who lived ages ago. The man helped mankind and was the enemy of evil forces. He was an inspiration to many magicians like me. But when he was killed, it was a blow to all of us. You see he died an unnatural death, but he will come back to life soon." The old man paused.

"How is that possible? How do you know that?" asked Andreux. He wanted to get away as soon as possible, but something was keeping him from leaving. The old man's voice kept him in a trance.

"I have spent most of my life in finding out more about the mighty lord. After he died, his powers were captured in this statue. I have sacrificed most of my worldly belongings in trying to get to this temple. My sole aim in life is now getting the statue back to life."

"You seem to be in fragile health," commented Andreux.

"Let not the physical appearance fool you, my child. I can do anything. Ask me for anything that you want me to do and I will show you that I can do it. Ask for anything that you think is impossible," said the old man.

"I don't believe you," said Andreux. "Your cascade failed in identifying me. You may have been powerful once, but it appears your powers are failing you now."

"That's impossible. The cascade never fails," said the old man. "Let me prove it to you. Tell me what you want to see. I can show it to you in the cascade."

Andreux wanted to see the tutelage. However he did not want his identity to be revealed. He was not sure if the old man was a spy of Nefarius. He asked the old man to show Senfred instead. He wanted to meet up with him again.

The magician got up with effort and walked towards the cascade. He touched it with his hands gently and put his face close to the cascade as he said, "Show the young man what he desires to see."

Immediately the cascade reflected a colourful garden. Senfred and Pompompulous were wandering in the garden. They were still discussing something very important, but Andreux could not hear their words.

"Where are they? I need to meet them urgently. I'm on an important mission," he said.

"Aren't we all!" chuckled the magician. "Your friends are locked in a trishank. You cannot find them that easily."

Andreux was crestfallen. How had they managed to get into a vicious circle? The forest was much more dangerous than they were told. "But you said that you could do anything. Can you please help in getting them out of the vicious circle?" he pleaded with the magician.

"I certainly can and will. But I have one condition," replied the magician.

"What?" asked Andreux.

"It is not that difficult a task, actually," said the magician. "I need the temple to be cleaned, so that I can prepare for the statue coming back to life. I must not use my magic for that. The temple, the statue and the pedestal—everything needs to be cleaned thoroughly, before I can start my work."

"Will you promise me that you will help me if I help you?" asked Andreux.

"I give you my word," replied the magician, running his thin, long fingers on his veined temple.

Andreux cleaned the temple. He used a broken branch full of leaves to sweep the dust and dirt away. Then he fetched water from a well that was behind the temple and washed the floors. He polished the mirrors and washed the statue as well. The brutality of the statue was no longer hidden to the naked eye. Andreux avoided looking at the statue. After he finished cleaning the last spot of the floor, he went to the magician. "I've kept my word. Now it's your turn," he said.

"Not quite. Not yet," said the sorcerer. "You have missed a spot on the pedestal. Finish that first."

Andreux bent down to clean the pedestal. He could not find any dirty spot. As he lifted a vine that grew around the statue and fell on the pedestal, he heard a tiny voice coming from somewhere very close. As he looked for the source of the voice, he found an insect crawling on the vine that he was about to pluck. It was talking to him, warning him, "The magician is a sorcerer. He is about to kill you. Kill him instead."

Andreux turned and looked at the magician. The old man now stood straight, his hands held a sharp sword. He no longer looked old or fragile. Just as his hands came down to strike Andreux's neck with his sword, Andreux moved away, pulled out his sword and deflected the blow. The sorcerer, who was not prepared for the counterattack, fell to the ground.

"Do not waste time, the sorcerer is powerful," the insect warned him again.

Andreux moved swiftly and dealt a decisive blow to the sorcerer's neck, severing his head from the body. The head hit against the wall and fell on the pedestal. His limbs shook violently and then his body became still. Drops of blood fell on the statue.

As Andreux looked at the lifeless body of the sorcerer, he heard strange voices all around. It was like the buzzing of a swarm of bees. Little particles of dirt floating in the air started to spiral around the body of the sorcerer. Andreux heard the words "Hail Levitor" and "Welcome back, O mighty lord." He looked back at the dead body and saw light and smoke escaping from the corpse. When he turned back, the cascade on the wall had disappeared.

If the sorcerer is evil then this statue that he worships must be evil incarnate, thought Andreux. He was not sure what this all meant. He hoped that he had not spoiled the plans of Veritus by not heeding his master's warning. Suddenly he realized that he had killed yet again. His hand hesitated and his sword fell to the ground.

"Oh no! What have I done? Is this what it takes to be a king?" he shouted, overcome with emotions. He fell to his knees as he hid his face in both hands and began sobbing incomprehensibly. As tears rolled down, he gingerly picked up his sword and looked at the bloodstains that now covered it. He wiped his tears and cleaned the sword with the sorcerer's robe before placing it back in its sheath. As he stood up, his grief was replaced with determination.

"I hereby vow to heed my master from now on and not make hasty decisions without acknowledging the possible consequences." Just as he said this, the ground under him shook violently. The explosion of the shelter was still fresh in his mind, so he ran out of the relic without delay.

The relic remained intact, however, and Andreux found another Capirona tree nearby. He looked around the tree to see if there were any hidden traps around it. Finding that there were none, he climbed it eagerly to see if he could locate his friends or find out how close he was to reaching Vauns. He found no one. However, he soon realized that this Capirona was the tallest tree in the forest. Remembering what the celestials had told him, he looked around to see if he could find his way to Vauns. The dark, miserable night slipped away into oblivion, and the sun slowly came into view. Andreux caught a glimpse of the fort of Vauns for the very first time in his life.

The fort, more than what he had been imagining over the past few days and nights, seemed impregnable, with walls that seemed to be reaching out to the skies. The gigantic stone walls had numerous security posts, from which guards kept their vigil. The moat that surrounded the fort appeared deep and wide. As Andreux sensed movement under the water, he recollected Veritus warning his group about the ruthless alligators that did not hesitate to feast on trespassers. The main gates were closed. However, there appeared to be a side entrance that served as a check post. There were not many people crossing the bridge across the moat at that time.

Behind the fort's mighty boundary wall, Andreux could catch a glimpse of the imposing palaces that seemed to be decked with gold and diamonds. The silk curtains adorning the windows were swaying gently in the morning breeze. In spite of the atrocities being committed by Nefarius, the city itself left a very favourable impression on the minds of visitors. Andreux filled his eyes with that sight. He looked at the fort for a few more monnets and he climbed down the tree.

"Senfred! Pompompulous!" he shouted excitedly. There was no response. He remembered the sorcerer's words; his friends were trapped in a trishank. Had the sorcerer been telling the truth? In the vision, his friends were in a colourful garden, which seemed out of place in the dark and dense forest.

What should I do now? Should I go looking for my friends or should I get to Vauns in time to meet with the royal prophet? Andreux hesitated. The words of Senfred echoed in his mind: "The mission is always more important than the mortals who serve its purpose."

But they are my friends and they may need my help. Andreux was conflicted. He recollected the countless yedibs that his family suffered in exile, waiting for this moment of glory. He could not fail his mother now. Yet isn't a ruler supposed to look after his subjects and keep their well-being ahead of his personal gains? After some soul-searching, he decided to look for his friends one more time before he entered Vauns.

But which way should he go looking for them? Again, Senfred's words came to his aid: "When in doubt, always keep to your right in the forest, so that you don't get lost in a maze."

Andreux walked to his right, deeper into the forest, calling to his friends. There were no signs of them anywhere. *Which way could they have gone?* he wondered. Just as he was about to give up hope, he heard voices above him. The lumen-drobs descended from a nearby tree and appeared before him.

"So what thought you about our offer so generous?" asked Ilvila.

"Your help they need; your friends are in distress," Fortuna said, teasing him.

Andreux's voice became stern, and he shook his fist at the lumen-drobs. "I warn you to get out of my way once and for all. Otherwise I'll have to take your destinies into my hands."

The lumen-drobs pealed with laughter when they heard his threat. "Threatens us, this mere mortal!" scoffed Ilvila.

"Yet he knows not, this is our portal," jeered Fortuna.

They raised their wands to cast a spell on Andreux, but he reacted swiftly.

He extended both hands and raised his palms towards the sky. "O Guardians of the forest! I am the Prince of Vauns, in exile, on a noble mission. I seek your cooperation. Thwart the mischief of these imps at once and restore peace and tranquility in the forest. Please help me." As he reached out to the forest and closed his eyes in reverence, a bolt of lightning flashed in the sky, illuminating the area. The lumen-drobs hid their wands and stepped back in fear.

The voice of the invisible force of the forest was stern and clear. "Leave this man alone or else you both will lose your powers forever." The light faded and it became dark once again. The lumen-drobs had disappeared.

"What was that light?" Andreux heard an unfamiliar voice in the distance say. He walked towards it, with his sword in his hand. He was prepared for any unwanted company. But the next voice that he heard filled him with joy.

"Be careful. We're getting close to the Ruined Relic. Master had cautioned us about the place." It was Senfred.

"Senfred, is that you?" Andreux said as he continued to walk.

"Finally! Where have you been?" said Senfred, emerging from the darkness. Pompompulous was to his right, and there were several other bandits with them. Sensing danger, Andreux pointed his sword towards them.

"There is no need for that my friend," said Pompompulous. He gestured towards the person next to him. "He is my father, Prosperus, and these are his friends."

Andreux was surprised. "Why? How? When did all this happen? The sorcerer told me that you both were lost in a trishank."

"Which sorcerer?" Senfred asked.

"Some other time. That's a long story. I'm so glad to find you both unharmed," replied Andreux. He then turned to Prosperus. "I've heard so much about you from Pompompulous. I'll never forget your sacrifices or the hardships that your family had to suffer on our account."

"My prince! We have all been waiting for this day for such a long time," Prosperus bent to take a bow when Andreux stopped him.

"I'm younger in age and experience. Treat me as your son's friend," he said.

"So be it," said Prosperus as he patted Andreux on his shoulder and gave him a quick hug.

"We need to get to Vauns in time," said Andreux, and seeing the surprise on Senfred's face, he realized what he had just said. "Yes! I did find the city from the top of a Capirona."

"How was it?" asked Senfred.

"You must see it to believe it, Senfred. It filled me with hope and inspiration. I'm convinced more than ever that it's all going to be fine from now on." And the group continued out of Aranya.

"What happened to Glimp?" Andreux asked as they finally stepped out of the forest.

Pompompulous and Senfred filled him in with the details of his misdemeanour.

"Looking back, I realize his loyalties had always been with Nevius. Yet we trusted him to accompany us," said Andreux.

"This journey has taught us many valuable lessons, hasn't it?" commented Senfred.

He knows exactly how to put my feelings into precise words, thought Andreux.

As they approached the city, Prosperus stopped them. He spoke to Andreux. "We must stop here. The guards know us too well to let you in if you are accompanied by us. Our heads carry rewards that are difficult to resist. We would gladly give our lives to you, but at this point in time it would be futile, as no one knows who you are. As such, no harm can befall you yet. We will wait to hear from you once you meet with the minister and the royal prophet."

Andreux nodded. "Once we reach Vauns, my master's orders are that we have to get into the city, one at a time. I will be the first one to go. Everyone else, including Senfred, will wait for his turn. We will all meet in due course," he said.

"May God bless you!" said Prosperus.

"Take care," said Senfred.

"Be ready with good news," said Pompompulous.

Andreux placed his sword in its sheath and walked towards the city. The bag of gold coins was secure in his cummerbund. The others retreated into the forest.

As he neared the fort, Andreux saw the guards talking to someone who had his back to Andreux. The figure pointed his hands towards the forest and the guards looked in Andreux's direction. They briefly looked at Andreux, and spoke again to the figure. When that figure turned to look at him, Andreux recognized him instantly.

"Nevius!" Andreux stopped in his tracks. He knew this meant unexpected trouble for him.

"That's him. Get him before he escapes!" shouted Nevius.

Andreux stepped back. The guards raised alarm as they grabbed their spears and rushed towards Andreux. Just as Andreux was about to pull out his sword from its sheath, he heard a gruff voice from nearby.

"Run towards the side entrance of the fort if you care for your life and for all those who have their hopes pinned on you."

Before Andreux could realize what was happening, several arrows flew out of nowhere and pierced the guards pursuing him. As their bodies dropped to the ground, Andreux ran towards the side entrance of the fort.

TO BE CONTINUED IN
BOOK TWO: NAMBUL